The Matchmaker
of Pemberley

An Amorous Sequel to All Jane Austen's Novels

The Matchmaker of Pemberley

An Amorous Sequel to All Jane Austen's Novels

By

Catherine Hemingway

Dedication

To Tamsin who attended the same school in Reading as Jane Austen and rekindled my interest in her writings with trips to visit her home in Chawton and burial place at Winchester Cathedral. I visited Bath when I attended Tamsin's wedding and I treasure all those memories more than I can say.

Chapter 1

Some might consider Elizabeth Darcy to have led a charmed life, not by virtue of an indulged upbringing, but rather by a propitious marriage. Even her husband on first meeting her had observed that based on her low connections, her prospects for marrying a man of consequence were materially limited. But that was all in the past, and indeed, her life was charmed in all aspects save one, the lack of an heir to the great estate of Pemberley.

As Elizabeth took a final glance at the contents of her trunk before it was loaded on to the barouche-landau, she gave a small sigh of relief. She had at first been reluctant to leave Pemberley for Bath, but Darcy and her father had convinced her that the change would do both her health and her spirits much good. She hoped their prediction would prove out.

Her sister-in-law, Georgianna and her younger sister, Kitty were delighted with the prospect of spending the season in Bath, anticipating exciting new social outlets complete with concerts, plays, dances, and expanded acquaintances. They had formed an attachment quickly in the days since Darcy took Elizabeth as his wife, and, in many ways, they were a good influence on each other.

Georgianna Darcy was shy by nature, having lived much of her life under the scrutiny of her older brother, who took over care of her and the family estate after the death of his father. She was eager to please, welcomed his indulgences with gratitude, and was greatly attached to Elizabeth, as the sister she had always wanted. In turn, the marriage brought several more sisters into her life including Kitty Bennet, a much more effusive and energetic companion. Kitty had benefited from the influence of her eldest sisters, whom she frequently visited, and spending time in superior society had improved her temperament and behaviour. Being close in age, she and Georgianna had bonded over shared secrets of past indiscretions in both families.

The delights of Bath awaited discovery and they were eager to get started. Elizabeth approached the trip with lower spirits than the young ladies, having recently experienced an early miscarriage during her first pregnancy. Her high hopes of providing an heir to Pemberley were dashed when, early the third month, she had been confined to bed and eventually lost this greatest prospect for happiness.

Darcy had been sympathetic and supportive, reassuring her that they would surely realise their shared dream soon enough and must accept the disappointment. The doctor, by way of encouragement, assured her that an early miscarriage in a first pregnancy was quite common and that she would certainly achieve her dream of bringing a child to term with the next pregnancy. However, he also suggested they wait a few months before trying again.

It was especially difficult because although she and her beloved sister, Jane, had married at the same time and even shared the same wedding ceremony two years earlier, Jane Bingley had already produced a beautiful baby daughter. They had always been the closest of friends and confidants, so Elizabeth rejoiced in the happiness of her sister and took delight in her little niece. Still, her own slow path to motherhood caused her deep sadness and concern. The pregnancy had provided proof of her fertility, but she had trouble overcoming her despondency at the loss just the same.

To raise her spirits, Darcy had suggested spending the season in Bath with all its diversions so she and the two young ladies were to travel together while he would join them in a fortnight due to business obligations in London. This would allow her more time for recovery and provide social outlets to stimulate her senses and restore her spirits. The excitement of the two young ladies had provided additional motivation to acquiesce to the scheme.

She surrendered herself to making the best of the separation and embraced oversight of the two young ladies in her charge. She hoped the delights of Bath would soothe her sorrow, ease her concerns, and rebuild her self-confidence, so she could finally realise her most cherished dream, that of producing an heir to Pemberley.

Darcy had already leased a suitably luxurious dwelling at Camden Place previously occupied by a baronet from

Somerset and they would be met by a Mr. Shepherd, who would introduce them to their new accommodations and facilitate introductions to the best social circles. Distractions and amusements were hoped for by all but Elizabeth, who would have been just as glad to stay quietly at home and take long walks in the extensive gardens and woods of Pemberley.

Parting with her beloved husband even for two weeks was a difficult choice. Their relationship had grown deeper in the time they'd been together, despite the impediments of getting to know each other when they first met. Each had judged the other as unworthy to be a life partner, and it had taken some time to truly recognise that they would bring out those traits most amiable in the other. Love had come slowly and unexpectedly, but once in evidence, had been embraced and nurtured. His dourness and disdain had been lifted by her spritely personality and good humour. She found her place in the world based on mutual love and respect rather than money and privilege, although the latter had followed the former.

"Oh, Elizabeth, what wonders we shall see in Bath," exclaimed Georgianna. "Just think of visiting the Assembly Rooms and tasting the mineral water at the Pump Room. Do you think it will taste strangely or provide cures for all sorts of maladies and ailments? I hear that people visit the hot springs and publicly bathe in giant vats of water with people looking down at them. Can you imagine such a thing?"

Kitty interjected, "What a lark it will be to visit shops and meet new people. I hope there will be many opportunities to dance at the Assembly Hall; Georgianna and I long for handsome partners who dance well. It will be so exciting, won't it, Georgie?"

With a blush in her cheeks, Georgianna nodded her head. "I do enjoy dancing but meeting new partners always raises my anxiety because I never know what to say."

"Don't be a silly goose. You need say hardly a word; just smile and nod your head. You dance very well and will attract the notice of all the handsome young men, but you must leave a few for me, for there is nothing I love more than dancing."

"I'm sure neither of you will lack for dance partners whenever the opportunity is presented but do contain your enthusiasm and not appear flirtatious or forward. You will attract all the attention you desire, for you are very pretty, young ladies, but must use good judgement as you meet new acquaintances. Remember, you are ladies first, well born young ladies, responsible to your family for your conduct and reputation."

Georgianna nodded her head solemnly in agreement while Kitty rolled her eyes and looked out of the window with a confident smile on her face.

While Kitty's deportment and enthusiasm for flirting had been subdued by the positive influence and close contact with her two eldest sisters, and her more conservative young friend, Elizabeth worried that the influence of her sister, Lydia, was still in evidence. Lydia, the youngest of the Bennet sisters had been overly indulged by their mother and become a renowned flirt, who cast aside all decorum and risked her family's reputation, to run off with her paramour, Mr. Wickham.

Resentment ran deep on Darcy's side. He and Wickham

had grown up together on the family estate, but their paths had diverged after the death of his father. Wickham, the son of the estate's steward, had chosen a path of dissolution: gambling, drinking, and carousing. Preying on innocent young ladies had been another pursuit and his efforts to seduce a very young Georgianna into an elopement had been interrupted when discovered by Darcy who then banished him from Pemberley permanently.

Wickham met the Bennet sisters when he was stationed with the militia in nearby Meryton and his attentions were first drawn to Elizabeth who, at the time, regarded him as a dashing and charming gentleman with whom she shared a decided dislike for Mr. Darcy, the guest of Charles Bingley, who was the newly arrived tenant at Netherfield Park. They were both wealthy bachelors and longtime friends, but while Mr. Bingley had immediately endeared himself to the local community, Mr. Darcy had been equally effective in offending everyone with his arrogant behaviour and disdain for his surroundings.

Mr. Wickham had an ingratiating personality and on first meeting Elizabeth, he eagerly shared stories of alleged abuse at the hands of Mr. Darcy, claiming he had been robbed of his inheritance. Elizabeth was already inclined to dislike Darcy due to an affront by him on first becoming acquainted with her where he had declared to his friend, Bingley, that she wasn't "handsome enough" to tempt him to dance with her and inferred she had been spurned by other men. Based on the initial insult, she eagerly embraced this new information from Wickham as affirmation of her own discerning judgement that Darcy was proud and arrogant.

As fate would have it, when the regiment to which Wickham was attached was removed from Meryton, his attentions were drawn to her youngest sister, Lydia, who had travelled with the regiment commander and his wife, to Brighton. There, flirtation turned to seduction of the frivolous young girl, who ran off with him, careless of the scandal that would be heaped upon her family. In the end, it was due to Darcy's intervention in both discovering the runaway couple in London, and making financial arrangements for them to marry, that the union was legitimised.

Elizabeth had no intention of allowing such a fate to befall Kitty or Georgianna and resolved to be on full alert to the attention paid them by new acquaintances, dance partners, and potential suitors. Kitty had no great fortune to offer, but Georgianna most certainly did, and would be an object of attention to many for more reasons than her beauty, sweet disposition, and talents. She would be relieved when Darcy arrived to provide support and supervision of the two young ladies with a wary eye for unsuitable acquaintances.

"Elizabeth, will we have to wait for my brother to join us before we can visit the Assembly Hall or the other attractions?" asked Georgianna.

"It will be very dull indeed to sit on the sidelines because we lack proper introductions," added Kitty.

"I can assure you that my thoughtful husband has already planned ahead for your enjoyments, including arranging suitable introductions to society, not to mention elegant accommodations," replied Elizabeth. "You shall not want for entertainments and variety."

"Do you know to whom we will be introduced?" asked Kitty. "I hope young men will be included so we have dance partners and I hope we have a chance to shop for new frocks so that we're fashionably dressed when we're at the Assembly Hall."

"I'm sure the dresses you brought will be quite in vogue, so you need not worry about your appearance. As for introductions, I have no idea what arrangement has been made but I trust in the judgement of my husband to ensure all will be handled with perfect propriety. He has our best interests in mind in all things," answered Elizabeth.

Winding through the Avon Valley and enjoying the early signs of spring, Elizabeth reflected on the unexpected path that brought her and Darcy together. As the second eldest daughter of a gentleman of property but modest means, there was little by way of fortune to offer any of his five daughters. With his estate entailed to the nearest male relative, their prospects of finding suitable husbands were hampered by undersized dowries. That the two eldest matched beauty with poise, intelligence, and good humour was to their advantage, but pretty women in search of husbands are always far more numerous than men of large fortune looking to marry.

Finding husbands for her daughters was the singular focus of their mother's life, and the greatest contributor to the constant vexation of Mrs. Bennet's poor nerves; a state of being that preoccupied her until three of her daughters were all married in the same year. The unpropitious elopement and eventual marriage of her youngest daughter, Lydia, had been a public scandal. The elevation of her two eldest daughters to matches that far exceeded their fortunes was to be celebrated, and no one revelled in their success in acquiring rich husbands more than Mrs. Bennet. That the first marriage had not materially damaged the prospects of the other two daughters was a miracle of love over commerce. The paths for both Elizabeth and her elder sister, Jane, to marry for love, had faced many obstacles, but who can account for affairs of the heart that bring young people together?

Elizabeth's aspirations were high when she took on the role of mistress of Pemberley. The sheer size and complexity of such a great estate that was already being managed by a large staff prior to her arrival required patience and good humour. Fortunately, she had long ago won the approval of the housekeeper, Mrs. Reynolds, and was quickly able to establish her position both there and at their home in London. The fact that she was adored by Darcy's sister, Georgianna, added to the felicity of all.

She knew there was outside scrutiny of the match as well, for many were aware her dowry was far short of the amount that would ordinarily be expected of a woman to marry a man of such consequence as Fitzwilliam Darcy. That it bothered him not she was grateful. That it was the subject of gossip or disturbed a few judgmental relatives or neighbours did nothing to detract from their happiness. That there would be people seeking to ingratiate themselves to the new mistress of Pemberley seemed certain, but this too would be managed with consideration where it was merited and good humour where it was not.

Mr. Darcy's estate was so vast that it encompassed several

villages and townships, each with its own parsonage to serve the spiritual needs of the local community. The living, with an annual income, was bestowed by the local estate owner to a deserving family member or respectable gentleman who had taken orders. Appointments were for a lifetime unless circumstances such as death or illness forced the vicar to retire, the only case in which the living changed hands.

Shortly after returning to the estate following their marriage and a short stay in London, an open house was held at Pemberley, to introduce the new Mrs. Darcy to the local community. Curious residents flocked to the event as much to visit the impressive estate as to meet the fortunate bride who had managed to secure the heart of the estimable Mr. Darcy. Among them was the Reverend Mr. Christopher Wink who availed himself of the invitation with great enthusiasm and deep gratitude.

Darcy had made several appointments since taking over the affairs of the estate including the preferment of Mr. Wink, a respectable, educated local man, to the living at Chatsworth, a small village on the southwest border of the Pemberley estate. He was the second son of a well-to-do landowner who had taken orders at Oxford; plain looking with a pleasing address, he had the air and agreeable manners that come naturally to the well born along with an overtly deferential reverence for his benefactor.

Upon meeting him, Elizabeth was reminded of another clergyman of her acquaintance for his obsequiousness of manner and open veneration of his patron. There was no more grateful a recipient of his appointment to the living and association with the great estate of Pemberley to be found except, perhaps, at Huntsford in the person of Mr. Collins, whose boundless devotion to his benefactress, Lady Catherine de Bourgh, was matched by the good fortune of being the designated heir of Mr. Bennet's entailed estate. His small conceits about his appointment and status had been amply on display when he first visited the Bennet family in pursuit of a wife.

Similar conceits were demonstrated by Mr. Wink, whose good opinion of himself was abundantly evident and buoyed his efforts to guide his parishioners in the ways of moral living, devotion to God, and service to the community. Instructing his congregants in the ways of the Church at Sunday services and performing traditional ceremonies celebrating village life provided an outlet to support his inclination towards officiousness, with his priority being to demonstrate unctuous deference towards his benefactor and, by extension, to the new Mrs. Darcy.

"Georgie, will you be trying the mineral waters at the Pump Room?" asked Kitty. "I've decided that I must try it at least once, just for the experience, even if I find it disagreeable, and I think you should too."

"I know so little about it," replied Georgianna. "I'm not sure what the benefits are although so many people partake of the waters that it must be of some value. I suppose doctors understand it better than we do or else they wouldn't recommend it. Perhaps we'll learn more when we get there. I dare say I will try it at least once just as you say."

Rising from her reverie briefly, Elizabeth said, "I'm sure it will do you no harm to avail yourself of the mineral waters and we will certainly have an opportunity to learn more when we arrive. I'm quite sure there will be many new experiences for us to encounter and, from what I understand, the Pump Room is the centre of social activity in Bath."

Returning to her thoughts, Elizabeth recalled her early days at Pemberley immersing herself in the rhythms of the estate, the grounds, and the staff. She devoted herself to establishing her role as mistress of the large household with its many complexities, and her astuteness of mind and affable demeanour soon won the respect and admiration of all.

She had been eager to explore and familiarise herself with the occupants who had been raised there and during one of her rounds inspecting the family wing with Mrs. Reynolds, she inquired about a room with an odd collection of furniture, near the chamber she shared with Darcy. This she learned had formerly been the nursery for little Georgianna, who had since moved to larger, beautifully appointed rooms. Curious, she inquired what had become of the nursery items, to be informed they had been removed to a large storage room in another wing of the house.

Given some directions and armed with her household keys, she discovered where it was located, and found her way to the storage room. She opened the door to reveal a marvel of objects including several old clocks that had ceased to strike, a handsome dimity bedframe, mahogany wardrobes with clothing still hanging inside, antiquated portraits, several storage trunks filled with linens and bedding, and, near the door, a small cradle with a carefully wrapped, delicately embroidered christening gown, and an ornate crib with a few dolls and toys piled inside, as well as a rocking chair. Elizabeth sat down in the rocker and picked up an old doll with a beautifully painted bisque face and hands. She cradled the doll and thought of that happy day sometime in the future when many of these items would see a fresh coat of paint and find their way back to the former nursery. Her fondest wish was to bestow a young son and heir to the Pemberley estate and make her husband the happiest of men.

Chapter 2

Several months earlier, Lizzy's younger sisters, Kitty and Mary, had arrived for an extended visit, much to the delight of Georgianna who had quickly formed a warm attachment to Kitty that blossomed into a fast friendship. Mary's devotion to scholarly pursuits and disdain for frivolity excluded her from their more intimate discussions and pursuit of entertainment. Although she shared an interest in music and performing with Georgianna, she affected indifference when the young ladies went into Lambton for shopping and socialising, preferring to stay at home reading, studying, or practicing. Mary's interests in reading, reflection, and musical pursuits left little time for the interests of most young ladies her age, such as dancing, shopping, and mingling with friends.

She was of a serious nature and valued educational pursuits and musical performance, although her intellect and natural talents did not quite align to her high-minded ideals or ability to perform. Lacking both genius and taste, Mary nevertheless applied herself vigorously and with far more conceit than her talents merited.

Evenings presented a particular challenge because entertainment by the ladies was often sought. Darcy's delight when Georgianna performed at the pianoforte' filled him with great pride at her accomplishments and he enjoyed it immensely. While his sister was often shy about performing, and would only play but not sing, Mary was ever eager to display her talents at both, thus disturbing Darcy's tranquillity. Her powers did not measure up to her delight in exhibiting, her voice struggled with pitch, her playing skills were laboured, and her manner affected. He revered his wife's talents and often entreated Elizabeth to join in performing for fear of Mary singing and playing all night.

One day Georgianna and Kitty went off to Lambton shopping, and Mary and Elizabeth sat quietly in the drawing room, the one reading while the other did needlework, when Mrs. Reynolds entered the room to announce that Reverend Mr. Wink had arrived hoping for an audience on an important matter of church business. Soon Mr. Wink was escorted into the drawing room and Mrs. Reynolds was sent off to arrange for tea. He was small of frame with a long face, pronounced ears and nose, and a disarmingly crooked smile. He bowed deeply upon entering and was received courteously.

"Forgive me, madam, for my intrusion. I hope my arrival has not inconvenienced you."

"You do not importune us, Mr. Wink; you are most welcomed. Allow me to introduce my sister, Miss Bennet.

Mary, this is the Reverend Mr. Wink, of the parsonage at Chatsworth, which borders Pemberley on the southwest corner." Mary curtsied, and Mr. Wink took another deep bow, murmuring his great delight in meeting her, and his extraordinary pleasure at having a second chance to discourse with Mrs. Darcy, the wife of his estimable patron.

"Do sit down, Mr. Wink. What business brings you our way on such a fine day?"

"As a clergyman, I consider myself to have a solemn responsibility to look after the spiritual needs of all my parishioners. My duties afford me the opportunity to commune with the highest ranks, with great humility of course, and with the less advantaged with equal felicity, for I am very mindful of rank and position. Every year the parsonage organises a local harvest festival and relief effort by collecting donations to help the needy of the community. Having been distinguished by the patronage of the most esteemed Mr. Darcy, it has been my singular privilege over the past few years to solicit support from my honourable patron for this most worthy of endeavours, and he has always responded with great generosity."

"It is a sacred duty to attend to the neediest among us and pour the balm of human kindness in the form of good works to bring comfort to those less fortunate," said Mary, nodding gravely.

"Indeed, Miss Bennet, you are quite correct, and it reflects highly on the benevolence and discernment of a refined lady like yourself," he replied with the utmost civility. "I cannot help but notice that you have been reading and must applaud your selection. Not many young ladies are interested in such noble and worthy books of a serious, instructional nature as *Fordyce's Sermons*. I must commend your excellent taste. So many of the young ladies these days prefer novels that excite unwholesome emotions."

"I always endeavour to better myself through study, contemplation, and good works," Mary replied.

By then the tea arrived and was served while the three discussed the upcoming event, to better identify the needs of the community and ensure how they could best be of service. Elizabeth closed out the audience with a promise to discuss the request with Mr. Darcy and arrange to generously accommodate it by the appointed date, after which Mr. Wink made a deep bow, expressed his excessive gratitude and the hope of seeing them again, pressing upon them an open invitation to visit the parsonage.

"Oh, Lizzy, I do hope we can be of some assistance to the Reverend Mr. Wink for such a worthy cause," exclaimed Mary. "It is the duty of those blessed with great abundance to be charitable to those less fortunate and I am sure there is much that can be done to help out," she said with great solicitude.

"I shall speak to my husband for guidance as to the nature of his support in years past, and I have no doubt that he will match, if not exceed his past contributions. I have another thought as well; as I have had the opportunity to acquaint myself with this great house, I came across a storage room with assorted trunks full of linens and wardrobes filled with old clothing. Perhaps you can assist me in identifying suitable items for the donation in addition to whatever Mr. Darcy recommends?"

With that, Mary gravely nodded her assent and smugly reached for her book, *Sermons to Young Women*, a compendium of essays dedicated to the virtues of feminine behaviour including mannerliness of speech and action, and modesty in appearance.

As the family gathered for the evening meal, Elizabeth spoke of Reverend Wink's unexpected visit and his pursuant solicitation on behalf of the parsonage. Kitty, disappointed at missing out on meeting a new acquaintance and burning with curiosity asked, "What can you tell us of his look and demeanour? Is his countenance pleasing and his address agreeable? Is he attached or still a single man?" she asked with a sideways glance at her friend.

Georgianna, being acquainted with the young man in question through her brother, replied that he was not quite handsome but, while agreeable, his manner was very formal as befitted his station in life. On hearing that he was unattached but having little interest in life at a parsonage, Kitty was soon diverted to other topics.

Darcy went on to discuss past contributions to support the charitable event including meats from the smokehouse, assorted preserved fruits from the garden, writing tablets purchased for the local school children, and a generous financial donation which he ascertained to be the most important of the contributions. At Elizabeth's suggestion he also acquiesced to donations from the storage room.

"Generosity and compassion for others and bringing relief to those who suffer, elevates both the giver and those blessed to receive, as it brings comfort to their wretchedness," said

Mary solemnly. "Mr. Wink must be a very good sort of gentleman to give such consideration to those in his care."

"Indeed, you are right, Mary, and with that thought in mind, I shall solicit you to help organise the effort to gather supplies so we can arrange to have them delivered in time for the event," replied Elizabeth.

"Perhaps we should plan to deliver the goods ourselves to ensure all arrives safely and show those small courtesies that reflect well on our commitment to ensure a successful event. I would be happy to exert myself for this most worthy of causes."

Mary's eagerness to comply with the request from Mr. Wink was matched only by her tenacity in accomplishing the tasks required. Darcy agreed to a generous financial donation that exceeded his contributions in years past, much to Elizabeth's satisfaction. He outlined the victuals that had previously been provided but as the process of gathering the provisions began, Mary was always quick to increase the bounty, asserting that compassion for the distresses of the poor was a virtue to be demonstrated by the generosity of the givers.

Elizabeth discovered her sister had natural organisational skills heretofore unrecognised as the visit to the storage room soon revealed. Mary was exacting in identifying cloaks, shawls, linens and listing the items, ensuring that even the storage trunks were included. The only things that were not up for review were the nursery items, although left to her own devices, Mary would have included them as well. Her assertiveness with the staff was unexpected as well, and she supervised the transfer of the goods to a staging area for eventual transportation to the parsonage. While Elizabeth would have been content to simply have the largesse delivered by servants, Mary persuaded her they should exert themselves and accompany the donations to their destination.

The day came and all was made ready, a note having been sent in advance to Mr. Wink announcing their pending arrival. Mary was in high spirits, which led to a state of enjoyment for both sisters; the elder observing with a smile that Mary was very much more animated than usual.

As the carriage left the highroad bounded by the Pemberley estate on one side, and turned down Vicarage Lane leading to the parsonage, they could just discern the neatly tended garden and the rectory within. Mr. Wink immediately emerged and greeted them at the small gate with an ebullient welcome and Mary flushed with excitement as the wagon full of victuals pulled in behind them and she recited from her list all the donations aboard. After providing instructions to the driver for where to proceed so the unloading could commence, Mr. Wink invited them inside the rectory with great formality and an offer of refreshments.

His triumph in hosting such consequential visitors was reflected by the obsequiousness of his civility. There could be no more grateful a recipient of the attentions of the two ladies, the generosity of their donations, and the condescension of their delivering the goods in person.

"I am overwhelmed by the bounty and beneficence of your patronage, Mrs. Darcy. That you do me the great honour of visiting me at the rectory, after being distinguished by the preferment of the living by your honourable husband, is highly commendable. As a clergyman, I feel it is my duty to promote and ensure the prosperity of all families within reach of my influence, even the neediest among them, and your generous contribution is most gratefully received. That you and Miss Bennet condescended to make the journey as well is indeed an honour of the highest order."

"Good works are their own reward, and we must all strive to ease the suffering of those less fortunate," Mary offered.

"Thoughts and deeds perfectly aligned bespeak your high moral character, Miss Bennet."

Tea was served and when they had finished, they were offered a tour of the parsonage including the small church. Upon entering the vestibule, Mary noticed a pianoforte' in the corner partially covered by a blanket.

"Is the instrument faulty?" she asked.

"I cannot say for I do not play, nor do any of our parishioners. It was a gift following the death of one of our most esteemed members, a widow who recently passed away. She was a great lover of music and since we did not have an organ, she graced us with this to accompany our hymns. It is most regrettable that we have not been able to put it to use."

Mary approached the instrument, raised the keyboard cover, and lightly ran her fingers across the keys.

"Oh, Miss Bennet, do you play? To be musically inclined is a gift from God for those who wish to raise their voices in His praise."

"I do indeed play. Along with my studies, I devote time daily to improving my skills, for there is always room to achieve a higher level of performance through practice. I believe in devoting myself to such pursuits whenever possible; if God has granted one any small amount of talent and inclination, one is duty bound to develop it."

"I'm sure you are much too modest, Miss Bennet. I would be eager to hear you play."

Mary almost sat down to the instrument, but Elizabeth thought the better of it and suggested there might be another time in the future to hear her perform. Perhaps Mr. Wink would like to call again at Pemberley some afternoon, to which he eagerly acquiesced and they settled on a day two weeks hence.

On the appointed date Mr. Wink arrived punctually, rapturous to have been invited to the prestigious home of his benefactor and eager to hear Mary Bennet play. Georgianna and Kitty made their excuses to visit a friend in Lambton as neither of them cared to watch Mary exhibit for the local clergyman. They were already privy to her performances, as she had been practicing two hymns tirelessly in preparation. Darcy found he had business elsewhere as well.

Mary was seated in the parlour when Mr. Wink was announced. She had carefully placed her volume of *Fordyce's Sermons* nearby and had a hymnal set up at the pianoforte'. She curtsied in response to his obsequious bow and invited him to sit.

"Miss Bennet, may I say how eagerly I have awaited the opportunity to hear you perform. It is a rare creature that combines musical ability with an ardour for study and learning. I see you continue to keep *Fordyce's Sermons* nearby. How very admirable are your efforts."

"You are most kind to say so. May I inquire how the relief effort that you organised turned out? I do so hope it was a great success."

"Indeed, it was, thanks to your tireless efforts and the benevolence of Mr. and Mrs. Darcy. It was undoubtedly our most successful event ever and raised the spirits and hopes of the neediest of my congregation. I am certain the blessings of the Lord shine down upon this house."

Elizabeth entered the room and greeted the visitor warmly as he stood again, bowed deeply in approbation, and repeated his acknowledgements of the great service they had provided. Tea was ordered and a discussion proceeded regarding the merits of each item that had been donated, how and to whom it was distributed, followed by his expressions of sincere appreciation which were issued repeatedly.

At last Mary made her way to the pianoforte' and announced that she had prepared two selections from the church hymnal that she hoped would please him. Her thin, reedy voice lifted in song and her fingers moved with rapidity over the keys, as she played rather better than she sang. At the conclusion of the first number, Mr. Wink was compelled to stand up and applaud with enthusiasm.

After she completed the second hymn, he felt obliged to state, "Miss Bennet, your performance was sublime! To think that you did me the honour of selecting songs from the hymnal. I am humbled by your thoughtfulness and greatly admire the meticulousness with which you play. Might I be so brash as to say that you have the voice of an angel that would elevate the sounds of the Cherubim and Seraphim in heaven. If

I am not too emboldened, would you consider coming to play for one of our Sunday services?"

Mary was overwhelmed by the invitation and her face lit up with pleasure, but she modestly replied that she was only in town for another week but would be happy to consider it during her next visit. She expected to come again at Michaelmas and offered to write to let him know when it was confirmed.

Mary did come back to Pemberley for Michaelmas along with her sister and parents. By then it had been arranged that she would perform at the parsonage and the family was obliged to join her for the service. Mrs. Bennet beamed with pride that day and following the service she effusively whispered to her daughter, "Lizzy, I do believe Mary may have found a suitor. Did you see how he looked at her as she accompanied the entire church in the singing of the hymns? Bless me but I do believe that I will soon be down to only one daughter in need of a husband."

Thusly began the courtship of two people perfectly suited to one another in temperament, way of thinking, and resemblance of character. Both reflected a sort of pompous self-importance matched with a false sense of modesty. When the Reverend Mr. Wink took Mary to be his bride, she moved to the parsonage where she immersed herself in providing musical accompaniment at all services and learned the Church of England hymnal by heart. What the parishioners thought of her accomplishments was a subject of much speculation between Mr. and Mrs. Darcy, but they were exceedingly grateful that their family worshipped at the parsonage in Lambton.

Elizabeth smiled as she considered her role as matchmaker. Unlike her mother, it had never been her intention to find a husband for Mary, but she had to admit that her ability to recognise compatible qualities and peculiarities of personality had been instinctive if not intentional, and she had merely provided opportunities for the happy couple to find each other. As she looked at the two young ladies sitting across from her, she wondered what fate had in store for them. She had no ambition to play matchmaker, but she hoped that they would find suitable partners and that her intuition would allow her to recognise and support true, honest attachment, because she loved them both dearly, and above all, hoped they would share the same felicity in marriage that she enjoyed.

Chapter 3

As they crossed the Old Bridge over River Avon and climbed the rise that eventually led down into Bath, a view of the city emerged, and Elizabeth was struck by the beauty of the architecture with tall, pale gold structures identically built giving the entire city a creamy, silky glow. Rows of houses emerged looking like wings of country estates. It seemed designed to delight the eye and promote a sense of harmony and serenity that she enjoyed as they drove the long concourse from the Old Bridge to Camden Place, their ultimate destination.

When the barouche and four pulled up to the stately residence, the door opened immediately, and a distinguished, fashionably dressed, middle-aged man emerged to greet them with great cordiality. "Mrs. Darcy, I presume. Welcome to Bath. My name is Mr. Shepherd, and it is my great honour to be here to greet you. Mr. Darcy specified that I give you a tour of the house and make sure that you are comfortably situated.

It is a shame he has been delayed in joining you here for what I understand is your first visit to Bath, but I assure you, I will do everything in my power to make you feel at home. Allow me to show you the house, for it is one of the finest in Bath, and I'm sure you will be delighted with it. These must be the young ladies of whom Mr. Darcy wrote."

He bowed deferentially as he was introduced to the Misses Darcy and Bennet. Upon entering, he bowed deeply again before opening the interior doors with a flourish of his arm, and walking triumphantly from one drawing room to another, remarking on the size of the rooms and the superiority of the fittings and furniture, all attributed to the refined, elegant taste of the previous occupant, a baronet from Somerset. Sir Walter Elliot had suffered the misfortune of a debilitating stroke, after only two years in residence. Every effort had been made to ease his discomfort, including frequent visits to the baths to hasten his recovery from the paralysis that afflicted his left side. As fate would have it, another stroke followed a few months later and he had passed away. The house was now the property of his heir, Sir William Walter Elliot, who had made the decision to lease it since he and his wife were currently residing in London.

Mr. Shepherd eagerly pointed out the arrangement of the pianoforte' that Mr. Darcy had specifically requested so that his sister could continue with her practice during their visit. The young ladies, having viewed the rooms and made their selections, were eager to walk off the discomforts of travel by exploring the town. Elizabeth, wary of letting them wander unaccompanied, was reluctant to agree, but Mr. Shepherd assured her that it was perfectly safe for them to use the pedestrian alleys and in a short time join the shoppers in Milsom Street. After admonishing them to return within the hour and gaining their agreement, she gave her blessing.

"Mrs. Darcy, I hope this wasn't too presumptuous of me, but I've arranged to make some introductions to people of social consequence, that I hope will enhance your enjoyment here in Bath while your husband is away. I'm sure the young ladies will be eager to visit the Pump Room and the Assembly Halls, and it will be so much more enjoyable for them to participate in social gatherings with formal introductions already in place.

"Lady Russell left her card by way of introduction and plans to call on you tomorrow morning. She is a lady of superior society and was a great friend and neighbour to Sir Walter, his wife, and their daughters for many years. She resides at Kellynch Lodge adjacent to the principal seat of the Baronetage, Kellynch Hall, and visits Bath annually for the season. She is eager to make your acquaintance as the new occupants of Camden Place and will be joined by Dr. James Baldwin, under whose care the late Sir Walter was tended following his impairment. He is renowned in the area as a doctor and scientist, greatly respected for his knowledge of the peculiar healing powers of the hot springs and specialises in the care of those seeking treatments for their maladies. He is the younger son of one of Bath's premier families and he will be a most acceptable companion when the young ladies enter society here in Bath. It would be very disappointing for them to visit the Upper Assembly Hall without proper introductions to dance partners."

"It appears you have thought of everything, Mr. Shepherd. I'm sure we'll be delighted to make their acquaintance and I thank you for your thoughtful consideration in planning for our comfort and felicity as new arrivals in the community."

Mr. Shepherd, with greatest civility, took his leave and Elizabeth could not help but wonder at the pride he seemed to take in showing the residence. Was it his connection with the deceased baronet; an association with someone of higher rank? There was a smugness, almost a conceit about his presentation that begged the question of how he could assume such authority of a property not his own. She was grateful for his effort to make introductions and looked forward to meeting Lady Russell in hopes of gaining a better understanding of his behaviour from her.

To Elizabeth's great relief, Georgianna and Kitty arrived back from exploring their new surroundings, flushed with excitement, eager to tell of all they had seen, and the shopping expedition they planned for the next day.

"Oh, Lizzy, we visited the most delightful stores and saw new frocks in all the latest fashions straight from London. There is so much more selection than in Lambton. We must plan to go shopping right away because Georgie saw a hat that she greatly admired, and another shop had a wonderful selection of the most beautiful ribbons. You must come with us next time."

The following morning saw the arrival of Lady Russell and Dr. Baldwin who were escorted into the parlour where Elizabeth and the two young ladies were enjoying tea. Lady Russell was an elegantly dressed woman of around fifty with an open, amiable demeanour. She expressed her delight in visiting Camden Place again and noted how little it had changed from the days when she had been a frequent visitor.

"I understand you were well acquainted with the former occupants," Elizabeth began.

"Indeed I am. The former Lady Elliot was a great friend of mine, and she was the reason for my relocating to Kellynch Lodge so many years ago. It was such a tragedy when she passed away, leaving behind three young daughters aged 16, 14, and 10. I endeavoured to provide the maternal support and guidance that their mother could not be there to give."

"Were the three daughters situated in marriage at the time of the baronet's untimely demise?"

"All but one, the eldest, named Elizabeth. The youngest daughter, Mary, was married to Charles Musgrove of Uppercross, which is not far from the family estate of Kellynch Hall. Anne, the second born, was married just two years ago to Captain Frederick Wentworth. They also reside in Somerset and we are extremely close. As it happens, when Sir Walter retired to Bath, Kellynch Hall was let to Admiral Croft, whose wife happens to be the sister of Captain Wentworth, a most felicitous arrangement as it allows for frequent family visits. Only Elizabeth, who was devoted to her father, remains unattached."

"Is Miss Elliot staying with one of her sisters?"

"Following the funeral, Elizabeth stayed for a short while with me, but then travelled to Ireland in the company of her cousin, the Dowager Viscountess Dalrymple and her daughter, Miss Carteret. They are expected to return to Bath soon and have taken rooms at the Royal Crescent for the season. The mourning period is now complete, and I expect Elizabeth will take her rightful place in society once again and will certainly be sought after due to her many desirable connections."

Dr. Baldwin, Georgianna, and Kitty had been politely taking in the conversation, with the girls exchanging glances as they observed the reserved young doctor. He was tall and rather gangly with dark hair and eyes, a full mouth, and a square jaw. He wore spectacles, giving him a serious, studious look. His dress was fashionable but had a certain rumpled appearance of one who is distracted rather than careless. Upon engaging him in the conversation, it was learned that he was the second son of a wealthy landowner who had been party to the revitalisation of Bath after the Roman ruins had been discovered and excavation begun. By way of introduction, Lady Russell mentioned that Dr. Baldwin was a scientist and tended to his research as well as the care of a few select patients, including Sir Walter when he had been stricken.

"May I ask how you came to pursue a medical career, Dr. Baldwin?" Elizabeth asked.

"Yes, I suppose it makes one wonder at such a choice. As a second son, I was expected to either join the military or take orders, but I'm afraid my inclinations leaned elsewhere. I've always had a fascination with the sciences and was able to pursue a medical education. I was fortunate that my father shared some of my interests, especially in geology and architecture. He was perhaps more lenient with me than most fathers might have been. Younger sons are usually dependent and expected to marry well but I'm fortunate to pursue my interests and live independently."

"Dr. Baldwin, what can you tell us of the mineral water served in the Pump Room?" asked Georgianna. "We've not yet visited but understand the water is served warm and has an odd taste? Is it safe to drink? Do you think it healthful?"

The question animated the young doctor and he leaned forward as he answered, "I highly recommend trying the water, but it is not to everyone's tastes. It has numerous mineral components, many of which we're still discovering. The Romans built the baths around the main hot spring around 60 A.D. but they were used by the Celtic people for thousands of years prior. Over time the baths fell into disrepair until a young chemistry and medical student, Thomas Guidott, wrote about the health properties of partaking of the baths in 1668 and rekindled interest. My own mother's relative, John Wood the Elder, redesigned the bath houses in their current style in the 1750's around the same time the bath chair was invented, which I make use of in my practice. The baths are just underneath where the Pump Room was built, and excavations of the ancient baths go on to this day. Do forgive me for going on." His cheeks coloured for a moment but his earnestness and enthusiasm for his subject added greatly to his expression and appeal.

"There is so much to be seen of Bath because of the great bounty of its natural resources. I would be happy to give you a tour if you are so disposed. We could start at the top of Beechen Cliff that overlooks this lovely city and then make our way downhill to visit the Pump Room and tour the excavation site to view the Roman ruins. My medical practice is focused on patients who seem to get great benefit from being immersed in the hot spring water. Sir Walter was taken there three times a week after he was stricken. My theory was to help his paralysed side to relax in the warm waters and slowly move his limbs to stimulate the circulation in hopes of improving his condition. Forgive me. I get carried away when speaking on these subjects."

By now, Dr. Baldwin had earned the interest and attention of Kitty and Georgianna who were eager for the tour and insisted on planning the scheme. The next morning was appointed for the party and Elizabeth was glad of it for, while she'd only been in Bath a short while, she was used to taking long walks in the country and already felt the confinement and bustle of the city encroaching on her. Climbing Beechen Cliff and enjoying the open air while viewing an appealing prospect was a distraction she welcomed. That it would entertain the two young ladies and increase the acquaintance of the young man was an added advantage.

After tea and settling the plan for tomorrow's tour, the guests took their leave with promises from Elizabeth to call on Lady Russell the day following the excursion. Both ladies were delighted to have made the acquaintance of the other and looked forward to their next meeting.

Chapter 4

When Dr. Baldwin arrived the next day, the barouche and four was brought out and the journey commenced to climb to the summit of Beechen Cliff. The prospect from the hill of the surrounding countryside with Bath nestled below made for a spectacular view and the city seemed to glow with warmth and pulse with vitality.

"With the sun shining as it does at this moment, the city seems to almost glow. It has such uniformity of structure as it nestles in the hillside and there is a certain gentility and liveliness to it all," commented Elizabeth as she breathed in the refreshing air and enjoyed the prospect.

"A keen observation, Mrs. Darcy," replied Dr. Baldwin. "The Ashlar stone itself is quarried locally and is so pale in colour that it does seem to glow, especially when the sun hits the pediments and cornices built into the architectural design. It was meant to align with the original ancient Roman walls, building on that heritage to give a distinctive allure as the city expanded. The stone itself is creamy and silky and it cuts beautifully. The masons find it quite easy to work and meet their exacting standards to achieve the vision of the city's designers. My father had a hand in the design as well and there was a calculated formula used to create the simple yet elegant look."

"How came the hot springs to be here?" asked Georgianna.

"An excellent question, Miss Darcy. You have an inquisitive mind. It is believed by scientists that a great deluge of rainwater collected as long ago as 10,000 years and sank below the Earth's surface, nearer to the Earth's hot core, creating mineral rich water that bubbles up naturally from the ground. Rainwater from the Mendip Hills filters through an underground layer of limestone travelling down about 14,000 feet where, by geological wonder, it is pushed back up through fissures and cracks in the limestone and flows into three springs. That accounts for the earthy tone and taste."

After a walk along the cliff to enjoy the prospect, the party proceeded down the hill into Bath to visit the Pump Room where people gathered to parade about, observe their fashionable fellow patrons, and taste the mineral waters by those so inclined. Kitty and Georgianna were adventurous enough to try and Kitty, after wrinkling her nose and swallowing it, determined she might rather bathe in it than drink it.

Next they made their way to the underground excavation site that revealed a huge rectangular pool with steamy, bubbling waters that were revered for the many healing properties. Some of the walls revealed ancient paintings dedicated to Roman gods and goddesses such as Minerva, who was once worshipped for her healing powers. As their excursion came to an end, they took their leave and spoke of perhaps seeing each other at the Pump Room the following day or even the Upper Assembly Hall the next evening. Elizabeth looked forward to her plans of calling on Lady Russell for she was eager to pursue the acquaintance.

Upon arriving home, to Elizabeth's great delight, she was greeted with a letter from her husband. She took leave and withdrew to her room so she could enjoy reading it in private.

My Dearest, Darling Elizabeth,

How I long to be at your side once again. Our separation has been most acutely felt, all the more because of leaving you to travel to a strange city on your own with our sisters under your care. Would that the circumstances could have been otherwise. The separation would be insupportable were it not for the important mission I have undertaken at your charge, and I am happy to report that the transaction is almost complete.

I will be forever grateful for the insights and clarity of your thinking that allows me to unburden my family's reputation by disengaging from a most shameful enterprise. Had we not discussed my family's heritage and one of the means by which we accumulated our substantial wealth, I might have long overlooked this stain. My great grandfather's investment in property in Antigua helped to advance our family fortune, but it was built on a vile practice of debasing our fellow human beings for profit. When I inherited the estate from my father, I became aware of the investment but chose to overlook it. If not for your good and wise counsel, I might have continued on that path even though it ran contrary to my own conscience.

This was a timely endeavour in two ways. I believe, as you do, that the tide will turn on this ignominious practice and see it banned from our shores, so hastening the demise of slavery cannot be undertaken soon enough. Coupled with the good fortune of finding a likely buyer of the property will allow me to leave this unfortunate segment of our history behind me. My solicitor, John Varley, has arranged for a transfer of the property in question for an agreed to sum. The financial health of the estate will not suffer significantly, and we will be relieved of the burden of profiting from the suffering of so many. Tomorrow I will meet with the buyer, Sir Thomas Bertram, a widower from Northampton, who already has holdings in Antigua and is predisposed to expand his investment there.

With that transaction completed, I will be free to join you sooner than I anticipated, which brings me great cheer, for I long to be with you again, and anything that hastens our reunion is an outcome I value beyond measure. You are the conscience of my soul and my heart's delight. I am yours body and soul and it could never be otherwise.

Colonel Fitzwilliam writes that he will be passing through Bath on his way to Bristol and will stop by for a few days until I have arrived. I am greatly relieved as he will provide you an escort to enjoy the variety of amusements available in Bath and help look after Georgianna and Kitty. He was delighted at

the prospect of spending time with you as he has always been
your great admirer.

I hope that Mr. Shepherd was there to greet you and
followed through with all the arrangements I requested to
ensure your comfort and felicity. He seems a very capable man
and he assured me he would make introductions that would
allow you to mingle in superior society while I am away. I am
anxious to hear that you are enjoying this sojourn from
Pemberley because I know how reluctant you were to leave.
Do not distress yourself, dear wife, with thoughts of the recent
past. We will be blessed soon enough with a child upon whom
we can shower our love and devotion so you must take time to
care for your health and recover your spirits. All will be well
and soon I will be with you again.

Your Devoted Husband,
FD

Elizabeth held the letter close to her heart and blessed her good fortune for finding a truly loving, wise, and caring husband. Who could have imagined such an outcome based on how they first met and the degree to which they misjudged one another?

Chapter 5

Lady Russell resided on the octagon at Laura Place, just down the hill from Camden Place and within easy walking distance. Elizabeth had insisted that Kitty and Georgianna join her despite their eagerness to press on to the Pump Room as she did not think it appropriate for them to visit such a public place unattended. They proceeded among the dash of carriages, curricle drivers, sedan chairs, and carts carrying produce which combined to create the din of commerce from shops and street vendors. When they arrived, they noticed a sedan chair on the kerb with two brawny men relaxing against a railing.

To their surprise on entering the drawing room, they discovered Lady Russell, Dr. Baldwin, and another woman introduced as Mrs. Smith. Although Georgianna and Kitty had been a bit perturbed at the delay in their plans, the delight at seeing Dr. Baldwin erased any thoughts of being importuned.

They were warmly welcomed and, by way of introduction,

learned that Mrs. Smith was a patient of Dr. Baldwin and had just returned from a therapeutic treatment at the baths to visit with Lady Russell. She had been a resident of Bath for some time having moved there to avail herself of the healing waters due to a severe rheumatic health condition that limited her ability to walk. It was revealed that she had been an older classmate of Mrs. Anne Wentworth who, at the age of 14 had been sent away to school following her mother's death. She was a widow when they became reacquainted in Bath, and following Anne's marriage, Captain Wentworth had been instrumental in resolving some business matters that had greatly improved Mrs. Smith's standard of living. She had moved from Westgate Building to Gay Street and having been introduced to the care of Dr. Baldwin, she asserted that she had benefited greatly from his ministrations. When she arrived in Bath, she was essentially crippled, but he had made great strides in helping improve her mobility. Lady Russell's and Mrs. Smith's mutual fondness for Anne had brought them together as friends and confidants.

Shortly after their arrival, Dr. Baldwin mentioned that his time was now free for the day and offered to escort Georgianna and Kitty to the Pump Room, a prospect that delighted them both. Elizabeth declined to join them for she wished to increase her acquaintance of the two women whose warmth, openness, and ease of conversation made her feel quite welcomed.

When the young people departed, their conversation turned to Camden Place and the former residents. Elizabeth commented that she was surprised by the number of mirrors throughout the rooms and learned that Sir Walter had been something of a vain man, enamoured with beauty, perfection, and his own superior taste. His eldest daughter, it seems, had inherited many of the same traits. He was said to have been a strikingly handsome man even into his fifties, and it had been extremely distressing when, after the stroke, the left side of his face had all but collapsed making it difficult for him to communicate. His attachment to mirrors had been thwarted along with his ability to move about. It had been a great blow to both him and his daughter who was not yet married and used to socialising at all the most fashionable gatherings.

When Elizabeth inquired about the heir, Sir William Elliot, she noticed a look pass between the other two women. It seemed that he was a cousin once estranged from Sir Walter and his family. There had been hopes that, when first introduced and invited to visit Kellynch Hall, he would turn his attentions to Elizabeth and take her as his wife. She was determined to marry someone of equal rank to her own and fancied the idea of keeping her name, the family estate, and continuing her current role in such a union. Instead, he had spurned the invitation and married a wealthy lady of low rank who later died but left him financially secure. Mrs. Smith and her husband had enjoyed the same social circles with Sir William, so she had intimate knowledge of both families.

"I understood Sir William Elliot to be married and residing in London," Elizabeth said.

"Indeed, he is. He was a widower who remarried shortly before Sir Walter's death and visited him while he was indisposed by the stroke," answered Lady Russell. "Having inherited the estate and being predisposed to living in London, he decided to continue leasing Kellynch Hall to Admiral Croft and his wife as well as arranging to let Camden Place, which brings us to the pleasure of making your acquaintance, Mrs. Darcy."

They enjoyed a lively conversation until Mrs. Smith tired and was escorted to the sedan chair waiting outside. She graciously invited Elizabeth to call on her at Gay Street and Elizabeth gratefully accepted. She had a feeling there was more to the story of Miss Elliot than either lady wished to reveal at that moment, but she hoped to learn more over time.

That evening they made their way to the Upper Rooms for the first time, no small endeavour in such a crowded place. The season was in full swing, which meant throngs of people trying to pass through hallways in order to join the dancers or achieve a view from which to watch. The press of people required them to link arms so as not to be separated until they reached an area where they gained a better view. Elizabeth regretted that they didn't have a male escort to help them safely traverse the room and find seats from which to enjoy the splendid sight. Kitty and Georgianna longed to join the assembled couples but, lacking introductions, they had little hope of finding partners.

After a brief interval, they were highly relieved to be joined by Dr. Baldwin who made his way through the crowd to greet them. He was accompanied by a gentleman who was shorter and of a stockier build, whom he introduced as his older brother, Thomas. The young ladies were delighted to increase the size of their party, especially if the addition included dance partners. The din of noise prevented much by way of conversation and when the next set began, they found themselves on the dance floor, Georgianna dancing with Dr. Baldwin and Kitty with Mr. Baldwin. At last they felt they had fully arrived at the ball. Their joy of dancing was short-lived however, for after the next set the music stopped, and the assemblage pressed through to the next room for the break.

Thankfully, Dr. Baldwin was able to secure a table for them and arrange for tea service. Mr. Thomas Baldwin was the elder son in the family and greatly enamoured with hunting and the breeding of horses and terriers, of which he spoke enthusiastically. He was an affable young man, less reserved than his brother, and the designated heir to the family estate. He was also an eligible dance partner and seemed well acquainted with other young men at the assembly, which bode well for continued opportunities to dance, once the tea was over and more introductions had been made. Elizabeth was very grateful that Mr. Shepherd had done them the service of arranging social introductions in advance, for it greatly enhanced the felicity of their first ball in the Upper Assembly.

Elizabeth would have been happy sitting at home reading, but she knew the importance of dancing to young women and men eager to make new acquaintances and Bath offered many such opportunities. Her own felicity was greatly enhanced when, to her surprise, Colonel Fitzwilliam emerged from the crowd to greet her.

"I arrived this afternoon and called at Camden Place to be informed that you were at the Assembly. In this crush of people, I can't believe my good luck in finding you!" he exclaimed with a good-natured grin.

"My husband wrote that you were expected in Bath. What good fortune that you were able to locate us. Where are you staying while you're here?"

"Sydney Gardens is a splendid hotel with wonderful amenities and I always choose it when I visit Bath." With that, introductions were made to the young gentlemen of their party and conversation continued until the music signalled the dancers back to the floor.

"How are you, Elizabeth? I know the terrible burden you carry in addition to travelling with Georgianna and your sister to a place you've never been. What a pity Darcy couldn't be with you to provide support. Yet I'm so very committed to his mission and applaud the decision. I have travelled extensively and spent a good deal of time in the East Indies. Colonialism brings its own forms of struggle for the local populations even if it doesn't export the labour. It is hard to turn a blind eye to social subjugation, no matter the form. Pemberley will be the better for divesting itself from the myriad cruelties, especially those that happen in Antigua. Please tell me you are bearing up with the change."

"I thank you for your concern. I confess the pressure has been deeply felt and it was a difficult decision to come here now, rather than waiting for the business to be completed. The separation was intentional to give me time to mend, body and soul, but it weighs heavily, and the confinement of city dwelling does press in on me. I have been fortunate to make the acquaintance of two respectable women whom I admire, and they have welcomed me most hospitably, but I long for a country walk in the woodlands and gardens of Pemberley."

"What say you to taking a walk tomorrow? I know the grounds and parks very well because I am a walker myself, as you know. Let me lead you on tour and introduce you to the bucolic abundance and beauty of the walkways and gardens of Bath. I insist."

"Very well, you have convinced me. You may lead the excursion tomorrow and we will follow wherever you take us. Tell me of your travels? Where have you been that led you to Bath?"

"I made my annual pilgrimage to Rosings which was a far less tolerable journey without the company of Darcy. Lady Catherine is much the same as ever and it helps to have a companion to absorb her pontification on all manner of subjects in which she considers herself to be an expert. She seems to have softened in her attitude towards your marriage which was a relief and I'm sure, in time, your presence will be welcomed again if not insisted upon."

"I would not be disappointed since it would give me an opportunity to visit my dear friend, Charlotte. Did you see much of Mr. and Mrs. Collins?"

"Quite regularly. He calls often and they dined with us several times as well. Mrs. Collins is delightful company and provides a welcome reprieve in conversation when Mr. Collins and Lady Catherine are otherwise engaged."

"And how is Miss de Bourgh? Is she well?"

"As well as she chooses to be on any given day. I don't wish to be critical of my cousin but I'm not sure if she suffers from a weak constitution that inhibits her activities or a general malaise of spirit. Her mother dominates every situation so it's difficult to determine to what degree that influences Anne's enthusiasm for society. There isn't much opportunity for her to express herself and little motivation for her to do so."

Elizabeth smiled and arched her eyebrows. "Has Lady Catherine alluded to her current wishes on behalf of her daughter? It would seem you are next on her list of desirable suitors now that I've married her first choice, to whom Anne was allegedly betrothed; planned from birth by his mother and Lady Catherine, or so I was told. Have there been subtle hints, or has she been more overt?"

"Subtlety has never been Lady Catherine's strong suit and she has admonished me more than once that it is time that I should marry and made clear the availability of her daughter and the desirability of a match for both families. She's gone so far as to send letters to my father in hopes of agreeing to an arrangement, so now I face pressure from both sides. It's a disagreeable vice in which I find myself placed, with both parties eager for my compliance and willing to exert whatever force they can to attain it. They are from a different era and think of marriage as a commercial contract to build family wealth and nothing of love and affection between two people. I must say I envy Darcy for choosing a love match after almost throwing it away.

"They are both forces of nature, but the worst of it comes from my father who would be equally content were I to marry Anne de Bourgh or Georgianna. It makes no difference to him so long as there is a great estate to inherit, or a very large dowry to be claimed. Can you imagine? I've known Georgianna since she was an infant and watched her grow into maturity; she looks upon me as a second brother. Even if Darcy were to agree to such a match, what would be the impact on her? She's docile and compliant enough that she would probably agree to anything her brother and I asked of her, but would that be fair to her? It's unthinkable. She should be free to choose for herself and marry for love although it certainly wouldn't hurt if her suitor also happened to be wealthy.

"How can I be expected to choose a partner for whom I feel affection but no love? I've lived in the world too long and witnessed too much to settle for a compliant wife just to please my family. My soul longs for something much greater, a wife to both challenge my mind and love me unconditionally just as I would do for her. I'm relieved to be here in Bath and away from the family pressures on both sides for they are too much to bear. This is a delightful place and I plan to enjoy all the entertainments available while I am here including dancing with a beautiful woman. I'm sure my cousin would never forgive me for allowing you to sit all evening observing rather than dancing. Will you join me, Elizabeth?"

With that they made their way to the floor and joined the other couples. Elizabeth was fond of dancing and grateful for the arrival of her husband's cousin. It would make their next visit to the upper rooms much more agreeable and she knew there would be high expectations of many such evenings, if Georgianna and Kitty had any say in the matter.

At last, the assembly dispersed after the dancing concluded, and there was more opportunity for conversation with Colonel Fitzwilliam, as well as room for the young ladies to promenade and observe the latest fashions on display, while feeling pleased and confident in their own elegant attire. Privately, Elizabeth could not help but be struck by the sincerity of his feelings and respect his position trying to withstand the unrelenting family pressure. It made her even more aware of the uniqueness of her own good fortune to have married for love.

Chapter 6

The excursion began when Colonel Fitzwilliam arrived the next morning. Exploring the grounds, the gardens, the crescents, the concourses from the Old Bridge to Camden Place was the mission of the day. Kitty and Georgianna's inclinations were for shopping and the Pump Room, but they were prevailed upon to join the expedition. They made the gradual descent from Camden Place to the Royal Crescent and then along the Gravel Walk through Queen Square down to Union Street.

They came across a great number of small delightful groves with pleasant vistas and charming lawns. These were intersected by serpentine walks at various turns with sweet, shady bowers furnished with seats for resting. Some included thatched umbrellas placed at equal distance from each other to provide shelter. When they reached Sydney Gardens, they found large pleasure grounds that included bowling greens, artificial waterfalls, a labyrinth, stages for fireworks and outdoor concerts. In all there were almost sixteen acres bisected by the Kennet and Avon Canal. It made for a charming walk and, while not offering the open expanses of Pemberley, it was a wonderful diversion for Elizabeth who would be certain to frequent them again and often.

On their way back, Kitty and Georgianna prevailed on them to visit some of the many shops. They entered the milliners to find new ribbons and enjoyed browsing while the shopkeeper packaged up a dress of the newest fashion for an elegantly dressed woman. "Mrs. Allen," she said, "you have such exquisite taste and I'm certain you will be much admired wearing this, for it is a true Indian muslin that will not go unappreciated by those who recognise its quality." As that lady departed, the new purchases of silk ribbons were completed before they made their way up the hill to Camden Place. A plan was already underway for another visit to the upper rooms that evening.

When they arrived home, to Elizabeth's delight, there were two letters just arrived, one from her husband and the other from her sister, Jane. She eagerly retired to her room to enjoy them in private.

My Dearest, Darling Elizabeth,

I write to inform you that I depart tomorrow to join you in Bath. The sale of the property has been completed and I am free to leave. How grateful I am that this entire transaction was completed ahead of schedule. It is truly propitious timing and a great relief to be able to rejoin you. I promise to make haste.

I hope to introduce you to a new acquaintance who will also be travelling there, a most capital fellow whom I met at the club. His name is Mr. John Willoughby, a highly respectable and charming man who was widowed a little over a year ago. He inherited from his wife, as well as property from his recently deceased aunt's estate. His marriage was short-lived for the saddest of reasons, when he lost both wife and daughter in childbirth. Please do not let this news make you despondent. I have every confidence that we will have many children to fill our hearts with joy and live a long and happy life together. You must believe that too.

Willoughby is no longer in mourning and a very eligible young man. That he is considered to be strikingly handsome assures that neither of our sisters will regret when he comes to call, for he cuts a dashing figure. I know you can read my mind so I will confess that I consider him to be a prospective match for Georgianna. I share your commitment that she should find a true love match such as we have, but there is no harm in putting someone highly eligible forward to see if natural attraction takes its course. He expects to arrive in Bath in two weeks' time and has promised to call.

I trust my cousin has arrived by now to provide companionship and assistance. He has been very supportive of the changes to the estate for which I am grateful since I highly value his advice and counsel. He is a well-travelled man with experience and knowledge on whom I rely as both a friend and advisor. I hope our time in Bath will overlap for he is always good company. I consider myself fortunate that he did not court you himself while I dithered with my pride.

Take care of yourself my darling wife and look for me to arrive on the morrow. I long to hold you in my arms once again, where no greater comfort exists for me in all the world.

Your devoted husband,

FD

Elizabeth spent a moment to savour the letter and the deep love and affection it conveyed. She was eager for his arrival, his absence made it feel as if half of her was missing and she looked forward to sharing the experience of Bath with him, creating memories they could savour in the years to come. Next she opened Jane's letter.

Dearest Lizzy,

I do hope you made it safely to Bath and are enjoying a beautiful new setting to lift your spirits. I've always wanted to visit Bath, but the timing wasn't right this year. Our own visitors have consumed much of our time and little Amy has grown so quickly that she is into everything now that she is walking. She is such a darling girl and brings us so much joy, but she keeps us busy just trying to keep up with her. Her nurse says she's never seen such a precocious child.

You on the other hand have had your hands full travelling on your own and getting settled in Bath with Kitty and Georgianna. I do hope you won't be alone much longer, especially now, while you are in need of love and support more than ever. I trust you are happy with your new quarters and have found pleasant diversions to occupy you. I am certain G & K have kept you busy exploring the city and its various entertainments.

Mama and Papa returned to Longbourn yesterday after a two week stay. They might have stayed longer but I'm afraid our dear mother's nerves were frayed from being around such a young child. How she raised five daughters with the accompanying noise and mess of little children is a mystery, but perhaps she had more patience in her youth. Still, she dotes on dear Amy when our little one is brought down in the evening before bedtime. Papa occupies himself reading in the study, so he doesn't encounter the childish outbursts as frequently, but in truth, I know he misses the Pemberley library.

Our parents overlapped by one week a visit from Lydia, and Mama was delighted to spend time with her. Wickham had business in town and didn't join us, for which I was grateful. Much as I endeavour to be patient, I find myself relieved when he doesn't accompany her since they often overstay their welcome and test my husband's good humour. As it is, she made sure I put something in her purse before departing. How I wish they would develop better spending habits and manage their expenses, so they live within their means.

I hope K and G have found many amusements to entertain them and had proper introductions that allow them to find eligible dance partners when they visit the assembly halls. I believe Kitty's temperament is much improved without the regular influence of Lydia, and Georgianna sets an excellent example for her to follow. Such pretty, young ladies cannot help but be admired and sought after.

Do write, dear sister, and tell me how you are. You have been much on my mind since you suffered your loss and the accompanying heartbreak that I know must follow. I cannot help but hope that travelling to a place with new distractions and entertainments will take your mind off your sorrows and that soon you will have your heart's desire. More than anything I wish for your happiness with the certain knowledge that it will match my own someday.

I remain your loving and devoted sister,

Jane B

Elizabeth smiled to herself thinking she was rather glad to be away, so the family party didn't progress to Pemberley from the Bingleys'. While she always enjoyed her father's company, that of her mother and her youngest sister could try anyone's patience, especially her husband's. At this moment, she was quite happy to be exactly where she was, awaiting the arrival of her beloved.

Lady Russell and Elizabeth had just enjoyed luncheon with Georgianna and Kitty near the Pump Room when the young ladies excused themselves to visit the Lower Hall to see what activities they could find. They would not be visiting the Upper Hall that evening because Colonel Fitzwilliam had arranged tickets for an evening theatre event, knowing that Darcy was due to arrive later in the day and would enjoy time alone with his wife.

As they sat enjoying their tea, Lady Russell was approached by an acquaintance, Mrs. Suckling along with Mrs. Elton, her sister. Mrs. Suckling was a highly regarded member of the community because her husband's estate, Maple Grove, was nearby and they entertained frequently. She had socialised with Lady Russell at various events during the season as had Mrs. Elton prior to her marriage. The two ladies were invited to join their party and Mrs. Elton expounded on her great fondness for Bath, not only for its proximity to her brother-in-law's estate, but because she met her husband there, before moving to a parsonage in Highbury. They had returned for a visit to Maple Grove and would be joined by their friends Mr. and Mrs. Frank Churchill, who were passing through on their way to Weymouth. There was great excitement that during their visit the Sucklings would be hosting a musical soiree in which guests would be invited to display their musical talents for the enjoyment of all.

"I have always been dotingly fond of music," enthused Mrs. Elton, "and I am uncommonly fortunate that my dear brother-in-law condescended to host a musical interlude in honour of our visit. We are so looking forward to the party and eager for the performances of the guests, especially my dear friends, the Churchills, who are most delightfully talented and exhibit great proficiency in both playing the pianoforte' and singing."

"Are you a performer yourself?" asked Elizabeth.

"I follow my passion for music whenever possible but will not claim to have true proficiency in playing the instrument, though my friends say I do. I have always immersed myself in musical pursuits and simply cannot live without music in my life. Do you play, Mrs. Darcy?"

"I'm afraid I confine my playing to family settings but rarely in larger social gatherings. My sister-in-law, Miss Darcy, is quite proficient but she is rather shy about performing in public as well."

"You must join our party, even if you don't perform, mustn't, they, Augusta? We'll send an invitation next week," said Mrs. Suckling. "I'm aware of where Lady Russell resides during the season, but may I inquire where are you staying, Mrs. Darcy?"

"My husband and I are at Camden Place along with his sister, Miss Darcy, and my sister, Miss Bennet."

"Camden Place is a very elegant part of town," murmured Mrs. Elton. "I'm sure we would very much welcome you to join our party at Maple Grove. People of means always make for superior society and I know my brother-in-law will be delighted to make your acquaintance. Do plan to attend and bring all your party along. It will be quite diverting entertainment, I assure you."

"I will discuss it with my family after we receive the invitation," replied Elizabeth.

After Mrs. Suckling and Mrs. Elton departed, Elizabeth asked, "Have you been acquainted with the Sucklings for very long?"

"We've mingled in society over the years but never formed a more intimate friendship. I dare say, Mrs. Suckling and her husband are quite amiable, and I became acquainted with Mrs. Elton when she stayed at Maple Grove before she married. She has always seemed quite enamoured with the status of her connections which is perhaps understandable considering that she moved from being a guest at a fine estate in Bath to an obscure parsonage; not quite as lofty a situation as that which she enjoyed living at her brother-in-law's. What say you? Shall we make an effort to attend? It will be an opportunity to expose your sisters to more of the best social connections in Bath and I'm sure they will enjoy the performances."

"I'll await the invitation and then discuss it with my dear husband. He arrives here later today and that is all I can think of for now."

Darcy arrived at Camden Place just as they began the evening meal. Colonel Fitzwilliam had joined them, ready to escort Georgianna and Kitty to the theatre, and all were delighted when he walked in the door. He rushed to Elizabeth and hugged her before greeting the others.

"Are you all gathered here on my account?" he asked. "I'm sure my arrival doesn't deserve such a show of attention, although I'm certainly delighted to see you all, and my timing is excellent as I find myself quite in need of sustenance after being on the road."

"Don't be too quick to flatter yourself about the purpose of our gathering," said Fitzwilliam with a smile. "While I am quite glad to see you as well, I am engaged to take these young ladies to the theatre to attend their first play since arriving in Bath. We've already attended the Upper Assembly several times so I hope this will be a pleasant diversion. Since you and Elizabeth have been separated, I rather expect having time to yourselves is a most desirable state."

"Fortuitous indeed, although I'm happy to spend time with you prior to the event and hear your news. What say you, Georgianna? How have you enjoyed your visit to this lovely city? I've always been fond of Bath myself although I haven't visited in some time. Has it met favourably with your expectations?"

"Oh yes!" exclaimed his sister. "Kitty and I have had a wonderful time of it. We've seen so much and learned so much, not to mention the gaieties of dancing and shopping. Everyone is so amiable, aren't they, Kitty?" she asked her friend, who nodded affirmatively.

"Well, my dear sister, I am intrigued that you mentioned learning over dancing. Tell me, what have you seen and learned that has made such an impression?"

"Dr. Baldwin took us on a tour all the way from the top of Beechen Cliff down to the Pump Room and then the excavation site of the Roman baths. He's a doctor and a scientist and very well informed. His patients receive treatments from the hot springs that feed the pools and he's done so much to help improve their conditions. He's a friend of Lady Russell's and takes care of one of her good friends, Mrs. Smith, who came to Bath in a crippled condition and, under his care, now she can walk. The ruins are directly under the Pump Room and are still being excavated to this day. We explored them and some of the walls are painted with Roman gods and goddesses. Do you know how the hot springs were formed? Dr. Baldwin says that a great deluge of rainwater collected here almost 10,000 years ago and then it sank below the Earth's surface to its hot core, and the water bubbles up naturally from the ground and later the Romans built the baths when they lived here."

"I say, you have seen and learned a great deal. I didn't realise you had such an interest in history and geology. What of you, Kitty? Were you as enthused with this tour as Georgianna?"

"I prefer shopping and dancing at the Assembly Hall, but I did taste the water at the Pump Room though I shall not taste it again. Once was quite enough even if it is good for you. The Roman ruins are, well, ruins, and a rather dirty place but interesting, I suppose, if you like history. But Dr. Baldwin dances well and so does his brother."

At last the meal was concluded and the party departed for the theatre leaving Darcy and Elizabeth alone to enjoy each other's company after their first separation since they were married.

"I dare say, I've never seen Georgianna express herself so unreservedly. What do you make of this transformation, my dear? It was most unexpected. Since she is of a marriageable age as is your sister, need I worry that she's enamoured with a poor country doctor doling out medicines and delivering babies?"

"On the contrary, my love, I assure you he is a most respectable and accomplished young man. He is rather shy and serious but is charmingly animated when discussing topics that interest him. He is the second son of a highly regarded, well-established local family that had a hand in the architectural design and development of Bath. His education and interests allow him to live independently and pursue his particular avocations which are quite varied. His older brother is very amiable as well, but his pursuits are anything but scientific. He is more of a traditional country gentleman with interests in hunting, horses, and dog breeding. I was so grateful to Mr. Shepherd for making introductions to Lady Russell and Dr. Baldwin, as it made for an agreeable transition entering local society. Lady Russell is a delightful person and has done much to make us feel welcomed. We have become fast friends already and I do enjoy her companionship."

"Your companionship is all I have need of right now, dearest Elizabeth."

Chapter 7

Although Darcy was no fan of a crowded, noisy assembly hall, the next evening found them in the Upper Room at the insistence of Kitty and Georgianna. While it was not an ideal place for conversation, introductions were made to Dr. Baldwin and his brother, who then guided the young ladies to the dance floor. The usually shy Georgianna was comfortably engaged in conversation with her partner, Dr. Baldwin, rather than exhibiting her usual reserve with strangers, which did not go unnoticed by her brother. They were soon joined by Colonel Fitzwilliam who shared his impressions of the evening at the theatre.

"Pray tell us, how did you enjoy the play?" asked Elizabeth. "Your guests last evening could speak of nothing else today and I thank you for arranging the entertainment."

"I'm glad to hear it. The Theatre Royal mounts all the most popular productions and the one last evening had a rapturous audience including your sisters who were greatly entertained."

Darcy arranged a table in advance, so when the break in dancing sets came, they made their way to the adjoining room for tea where conversation would be somewhat easier. Dr. Baldwin and his brother joined them and while Dr. Baldwin was engaged talking to Darcy, Mr. Thomas Baldwin introduced Georgianna and Kitty to his friends visiting from Oxford, Mr. John Thorpe and Mr. James Morland saying, "Mr. Thorpe is pressing me to purchase a fine young colt that he won in a card game claiming it will be a great investment. What do you ladies recommend?"

"If it will add felicity to your life and you can afford the care and feeding then by all means you should," replied Kitty.

"There you go, Baldwin! Listen to Miss Bennet. I guarantee this colt will add to your felicity while it also helps my pocketbook," laughed Mr. Thorpe. "A win for us both, and I'll throw in one of my terrier pups in the bargain. My bitch whelped a litter and I already have my friend, Charles Musgrove of Uppercross, in line to take one of them once they're weaned."

Overhearing their conversation, Elizabeth asked if Mr. Musgrove was the husband of the youngest daughter of Sir Walter Elliot, which was quickly affirmed.

"Indeed, Mr. Musgrove is the very same. He's an excellent shot, rides well, and he has a fine eye for terriers to add to his breeding stock, while Mr. Baldwin will benefit twice over in the bargain if he takes this colt off my hands," replied Mr. Thorpe.

To this Mr. Baldwin replied that he would ride out and look

at the animal before he decided on the offer. Mr. Thorpe then asked Miss Bennett for the next dance as a means of thanking her for her contribution to the negotiation which was a less than satisfactory outcome for Mr. Baldwin who had hoped the next dance would be his, as well as for Kitty who far preferred the company of Mr. Baldwin to that of Mr. Thorpe whom she considered to be rather brusque and not in the least bit handsome.

Colonel Fitzwilliam and Elizabeth were engaged in conversation when he was startled by the approach of an old acquaintance. "Brandon! Is it really you? By God, it's been a long time my good man. I haven't seen you since we served in the East Indies together. Where do you reside now and what brings you to Bath?"

Colonel Brandon and his wife were introduced to the party and Elizabeth engaged Mrs. Marianne Brandon in conversation which allowed the two former officers of the regiment to exchange stories of their past service together and discuss their current pastimes. For both women, it was their first visit to Bath, each having been there only a short time, so they had much to exchange and discuss about their experiences. The Brandons lived at Delaford, near Barton and were on holiday, intending to travel to Weymouth after their stay in Bath. The sets commenced again and at the end of the evening it was decided that a dinner party would be arranged the following week to include Colonel Fitzwilliam, Colonel Brandon and his wife, Marianne, as well as Lady Russell who had yet to be introduced to Mr. Darcy.

Later that evening Elizabeth and Darcy discussed the new

acquaintances including Dr. Baldwin and his brother as well as the Brandons.

"Mrs. Brandon is such a charming woman, so young and attractive. No wonder Colonel Brandon was smitten with her but there is such an age difference that I wonder what the attraction was for her," commented Elizabeth.

"Wealth and comfort account for many such matches," replied Darcy, "although I hesitate to assume that there weren't other inducements for an attachment based on more meaningful attractions. He's clearly enamoured but she seems to dote on his attentions as well."

"I do look forward to getting to know her better and I understand from her husband that she is a gifted pianist and that will bring great enjoyment to Georgianna."

"Speaking of my sister, what am I to make of a seeming attachment to Dr. Baldwin or am I imagining that she is smitten? I've rarely seen her engage in conversation so unreservedly, he was very attentive to her, and might I add, they danced several dances together this evening. Have I cause for concern? I have far higher aspirations for her than attaching herself to a country doctor."

"I'm sure it's nothing serious, my dearest, but she does seem to have developed an interest in science and history that is most unexpected. She so enjoys listening to him and absorbs the information he shares with enthusiasm. I never imagined her interests would lean in such a direction."

"So long as she doesn't lean any further than expanding her mind rather than towards forming an attachment."

"Would that really be so bad? We've often said that we wish

for her a love match such as our own so she could experience the same happiness we enjoy despite our fractious beginning."

"That is all well and good, but it is my duty as her brother to ensure a proper match for her, suitable to her station in life. I have high expectations and intend to introduce her to the society of her equals from whom she can then choose to fall in love."

On the evening of the dinner party, the Brandons and Colonel Fitzwilliam arrived together followed shortly by Lady Russell. When Mrs. Brandon entered the drawing room she exclaimed, "A pianoforte'! How delightful. I must say that the only thing I truly miss when travelling is an instrument to play."

"Mr. Darcy arranged for it when he made our travel plans so that Georgianna could continue her practice while we are situated here. I take it you are a music lover and performer?"

"I confess that I take greater pleasure in playing than performing. Some part of every day is occupied by the sublime pleasure of playing favourites and learning new ones. I have no need of an audience to feel compelled to sit and experience the rapture of beautiful melodies by favourite composers."

"That settles it then, we shall entertain each other this evening. I know Georgianna will enjoy listening to you and exhibiting her own proficiency. And, while you're in town, you must plan to come every day that you are free of other engagements so that you can play. Anyone so devoted to music as you should have as much opportunity as possible."

"If you are certain that it wouldn't importune you, I gladly accept your offer. It always lifts my spirits when I play, and I have greatly missed the opportunity. You are most kind and considerate to offer."

The evening entertainment went splendidly. Georgianna played very well despite her usual shyness, Elizabeth took a turn, and then the two played a duet. When Marianne sat down to the instrument she played with energy and deep emotion, holding her audience enraptured, especially her husband, who looked on with great pride and obvious affection. Despite the age difference between them, there was great mutual warmth and regard. Elizabeth was delighted with her new acquaintances.

Lady Russell and Darcy engaged in a lively conversation about the former occupants of Camden Place and the extended family with whom she was still so closely attached. Having overheard some of their discussion, Elizabeth determined to follow through on her plans to visit Mrs. Smith presently, as she felt certain there must be more to the story of the Elliots' recent history and could not contain her curiosity, especially knowing she would soon meet Miss Elizabeth Elliot. At the end of the evening Lady Russell declared it was one of the best musical performances she had ever had the pleasure of witnessing.

Marianne did take Elizabeth up on her offer and came most mornings when the men were likely to be out and about. One of those mornings there was a knock at the door, and who should enter the parlour but Mrs. Suckling and Mrs. Elton come to deliver their invitation to the upcoming musical soiree at Maple Grove. Apologising for the intrusion, they were introduced to Mrs. Brandon and then the two new guests began admiring the drawing rooms and remarking on the size and elegance of the arrangement.

"What splendid rooms and beautifully appointed,"

remarked Mrs. Suckling. "Camden Place is such a delightful location, very prestigious; don't you agree, Augusta?"

"Oh, indeed I do. I have always believed that superiority in taste reflects superiority of mind. And look, how fortunate to have a pianoforte so conveniently located for entertainment. We could not help but hear music playing when we arrived. Pray, was that you, Mrs. Darcy or your guest, Mrs. Brandon?"

When informed that it was Marianne at the instrument, Mrs. Elton declared, "We are mortified to have interrupted any sort of musical performance and hope you will continue playing despite our arrival. The dulcet tones of a pianoforte' in gifted hands elevates and gratifies all who are privileged to hear it."

"Perhaps after tea is served," replied Mrs. Brandon, who did return to the instrument again later, after which Mrs. Elton declared she was thoroughly enraptured with the performance.

"I do so appreciate your selection of music, Mrs. Brandon. I take extreme interest in the selection of composers and sublime pleasure in hearing them performed. I don't claim to be an aficionado of great musical compositions, although my friends say I am. It would be such a delight if you would join us next week for the musical soiree taking place at Maple Grove. All the best people will be there and I'm sure there will be superior performances all round for us to enjoy. You will be delighted with my dear friends, Mr. Frank Churchill and his wife, Jane, who are marvellous performers."

Upon inquiring about the length of their intended stay and their location in town, Mrs. Suckling extended the invitation to the Brandons to attend the musical event at Maple Grove as well. "I shall have an invitation delivered to Sydney Gardens this very afternoon and you shall have a Broadwood Grande at your disposal, for my husband always chooses superior quality instruments for our home."

Once the unexpected guests had departed, Elizabeth observed to Marianne, "I'm afraid Mrs. Suckling and Mrs. Elton appear to be rather pretentious, and I have no wish for them to importune you. Out of courtesy to Lady Russell we shall probably attend their party, but please don't feel any sense of obligation to do so yourself unless it will add to the felicity of your visit. Since my husband has only recently arrived, I've not had an opportunity to speak to him about the invitation, but it's another opportunity for our younger sisters to mingle in society and I shall hold out hope that the musical performances meet the lofty tastes of Mrs. Elton."

Marianne smiled. "I'm sure we have nothing more pressing on our schedule and the superior sound produced by a Broadwood Grande is a most attractive inducement. I will take it up with my husband as well, and so long as Colonel Fitzwilliam is in attendance, I'm sure he will have no objection. They take great enjoyment in discussing their past travels and exploits. My husband, who is rather reserved by nature, appears much more animated when discussing life in the regiment. It does him good and I cannot object to any opportunity to play so long as the instrument is well tuned."

"In that case, we will gladly attend. I am already a great admirer of your talents and I'm sure Georgianna cannot help but be influenced by your example. We shall make it a party."

Chapter 8

"So good of you to call on me, Mrs. Darcy," enthused Mrs. Smith. "I am indeed honoured and how very propitious! I've only just arrived home from my spa therapy with Dr. Baldwin this morning. Please forgive me for not rising to greet you, but I am under express orders to limit my activities after my sessions and I am so grateful to be under the care of the good doctor, for he has certainly worked miracles in my life, that I fully commit to obeying his orders."

Elizabeth had looked forward to visiting Mrs. Smith for some time. She was already fond of Lady Russell and understood that the friendship developed between the two women was based on an intimate connection with Mrs. Anne Elliot Wentworth, with whom both had long-established relationships. Mrs. Smith's connection dated back to school days whilst Lady Russell's extended even further to Anne's early childhood. Their relationship was evidence that Mrs.

Smith was an open, intelligent, respectable woman worthy of being called a friend.

Under the care of Dr. Baldwin, her health had improved considerably, which was certainly a testament to him but also to her own fortitude and cheerfulness. Elizabeth had developed great respect and admiration for the young doctor based on the unique remedies he provided by exploring the physical universe of science and applying it to therapeutic treatments. That he was a favourite of Georgianna and Kitty and was amiable company in his own right increased the felicity of all.

"You are fortunate indeed to have such an accomplished and forward-thinking medical practitioner. Was your introduction to him the result of his effort to treat Sir Walter Elliot after he was stricken?"

"Yes, Lady Russell introduced us when she learned of my rheumatic condition, for which I will be forever grateful. I had tried to avail myself of the healing waters like so many others, but under his direct care my condition improved measurably. They have both become friends that I treasure."

"I don't wish to importune you, but may I inquire further about the aftermath of Sir Walter's death? I can't help but wonder about the outcome for his oldest daughter, Miss Elliot. Why did she not continue residing at Camden Place?"

"How much time do you have for this visit?" laughed Mrs. Smith. "It is a long story, but you surely have a right to hear it as you will certainly meet Miss Elliot someday soon and will uncover at least some of the recent history. But allow me to take you back further in the story as my connection with the family members requires it.

"I met dear Anne Elliot when she was sent away to school following her mother's death at the age of 14. She was so despondent and I, being a few years older, took her under my wing. Our paths diverged when I left school and married my husband, Charles, whose fortune allowed us to live in a very good style in town. Mr. William Elliot, Sir Walter's cousin and heir, was my husband's intimate friend since before our marriage and he embraced me as a confidant. At the time he was rather impoverished but made every effort to look the gentleman aided by the generosity of my husband.

"Mr. Elliot told me about his initial introduction to Sir Walter and his daughter, Elizabeth, and expressed his complete and utter disdain for them both. He was aware that he was to inherit Kellynch Hall, and they were in hopes that he would court Elizabeth and make her the next Lady Elliot, but he was of no mind to live poorly while he awaited an inheritance, nor could he abide the insufferable vanity of the two. He was determined to make his fortune by marrying it and found a well-situated woman of lower rank whom he charmed into marriage to make his stake.

"After the marriage, his spending was profligate at the expense of his wife whom he treated with as much disdain as he did his future inheritance. My husband attempted to keep pace but unfortunately overextended his commitments and upon his untimely death, despite all the generosity he had demonstrated to Mr. Elliot in earlier times, I was left in difficult financial circumstances with no hope of extrication. Mr. Elliott could have lent a hand in a business matter to help secure my comfort and solace but instead I have Captain

Wentworth to thank for interceding in a claim on my behalf which allows me the small comforts I now enjoy."

"I'm shocked indeed to hear of such callousness. Did he remain aloof until after the death of Sir Walter?" asked Elizabeth.

"On the contrary, he came to realise the risk to his inheritance when he received word from a friend that the Elliots had arrived in Bath accompanied by the daughter of their lawyer, Mr. Shepherd, a Mrs. Clay, whom Elizabeth befriended over her own sister, dear Anne. Only then did he insert himself into their lives as a means of ascertaining the extent of Mrs. Clay's influence and craft.

"Lady Russell and Anne were both concerned that Mrs. Clay's assiduous attentions to Elizabeth and her father were predicated on the hope of someday becoming Lady Elliot, by ingratiating herself to them both and eventually winning the heart of Sir Walter. Their vanity was such that neither could see the artifice behind her art of pleasing nor contemplate such an outcome as even a remote possibility. After all, Sir Walter had stayed single such a long time for his daughters' sake. However, when Mr. Elliot got wind of the situation through his friend, he travelled to Bath to establish whether there might be an actual threat to his inheritance. By then he was a wealthy widower and more favourably disposed towards the prospect of assuming the dignity of being baronet with a prosperous and respectable family history. He was not about to let someone as unequal in rank as Mrs. Clay orchestrate a degrading match with Sir Walter and possibly produce an heir.

"When he arrived, Mr. Elliot begged forgiveness for his

past transgressions and ingratiated himself in every way by visiting Camden Place frequently to court the goodwill of the family and establish whether Mrs. Clay was being effective in her efforts to secure the attentions of Sir Walter.

"Now I must share another piece of this intrigue. The reason the Elliots moved to Bath was to contain the extravagances of Sir Walter and his daughter and to repair their debts. Rather than choosing moderation and economy as the means to overcome their financial stress, they chose to relocate to Bath and lease the family estate to Admiral Croft. It was hoped that this economising would allow the estate to pay back creditors over the course of seven years. Bath was chosen as a place where Sir Walter could maintain his consequence in society at reduced expense and thus retire his debts. That Lady Russell spent the season here annually added to the felicity of the arrangement. Only Anne was not eager for the move as she had advocated for economising instead, but at last she was prevailed upon to support the plan.

"Anne had been left behind to oversee the final details of the move and then to visit her younger sister, Mary Musgrove, at Uppercross. There she became reacquainted with Captain Wentworth, to whom she had once been greatly attached, for when she was 19, they had been engaged. Upon hearing the news, Sir Walter demanded an end to the arrangement because Captain Wentworth lacked fortune and consequence and she was forced to give him up. To make matters worse, he was also the brother of Mrs. Croft whose husband, the admiral, had just let Kellynch Hall. It was an awkward reunion after eight years' separation and her current displacement."

"When Mr. Elliot reintroduced himself to Sir Walter, did he pursue the courtship of Miss Elliot?"

"Oh dear, on the contrary. He still despised her vanity and when Anne, who was an intelligent, pretty, and modest young woman, finally arrived in Bath, he set his sights on securing her hand instead and he almost succeeded. He pursued her with true interest and honest affection, to the degree he was capable of either. However, his plans were thwarted when the long-delayed affection between Captain Wentworth and Anne rekindled. With the announcement of their intention to marry, he quit Bath immediately."

"Was he not still concerned about a potential attachment forming between Mrs. Clay and Sir Walter?"

"The news of the engagement destroyed Mr. Elliot's plans for domestic happiness, but the always resourceful man had been at work capturing the affections of another, those of Mrs. Clay! When he quit Bath, so did she shortly thereafter, and it was said he had taken her under his protection and installed her in an apartment in London, presumably to prevent her continuing her effort to win over Sir Walter and produce an heir. His artfulness almost exceeded her own. She gave up her schemes for the one but not the other.

"When Sir Walter was stricken, Elizabeth sent for Anne immediately. She was beside herself over what to do and horrified by the visage of her father. They had both long disdained any physical imperfections in others and now, here he was, immobilised and unable to speak with the left side of his body locked in an awful, paralysed condition. She could not bear to look at him and knew not what to do.

"By the time Anne arrived, Elizabeth had seized upon a plan from which she would not relinquish herself. She had determined to write to Mr. Elliot to inform him of the tragic event and invite him to visit her father one more time. Although she knew he had favoured Anne over herself, she was convinced that she could win him yet. Once arrived, she would shower him with attention and demonstrate her devotion to her father as an example of her loyal and loving nature. She was sure he would recognise her as the true and natural mistress of Kellynch Hall, with all the graces and airs that such a role required. She had designs for taking him into society to showcase her many charms and suitability as a wife. She had also grown fatigued of staying at home with her invalid, immobilised, and disfigured father when she was used to being out in society.

"When informed of her plans, Anne begged Elizabeth not to pursue the scheme, for Anne had a far better idea of the character of Mr. Elliot than did her sister, as well as his history of repugnance for both father and daughter. She had read it in a letter written to me many years earlier by Mr. Elliot when my husband was still alive. I shared it with her after we became reacquainted in Bath, and only after I was reassured she had no attachment to him. Anne said, 'Please reconsider your plan, Elizabeth. No good can come of it. He's had many opportunities to observe your qualities and has no history of responding favourably to your charms'.

"She replied, 'You just mean to discourage me because you already have a husband. You overthrew Mr. Elliot in favour of Captain Wentworth, which was entirely inexplicable, and now you resent similar happiness for me. Well, you are too late. I've already sent the letter and expect Mr. Elliot to arrive presently. I mean to show him all the courtesies and entertainments that he could expect in a wife and prepare him for the potential loss of our dear father to whom he was so very attached'.

"The day did arrive that brought Mr. Elliot to Camden Place but he was not alone. When he entered the parlour, he was greeted enthusiastically by Elizabeth and thanked profusely for coming, until she saw who stood behind him, none other than Mrs. Clay.

"She exclaimed, 'Mrs. Clay, this is a surprise. What brings you to Bath?'

"'I'm here with my husband for I am now Mrs. William Elliot. We were married quite recently. I surmise you have not heard the news?'

"With that announcement, Elizabeth was so taken aback that she had to excuse herself and leave the room, such was the nature of her shock. Anne did her best to welcome them and invited them to sit but the new Mrs. Elliot chose to stroll around the parlour admiring the furnishings and decorations.

"'Dear Sir Walter, he always had such exquisite taste and demonstrated superior knowledge of all things rare and beautiful. I shall forever be grateful for my exposure to the finer things in life under his gracious guidance. I remember the day he purchased this clock; his discernment in discovering treasures of superior quality was such a gift. How does he fare, Mrs. Wentworth? We're quite concerned about his condition, aren't we my dear?'

"'Indeed, we are,' replied Mr. Elliot. 'Will we be able to see him today to give him our regards and best wishes for a full recovery?'

"'His man servant is preparing him for the day,' Anne responded. 'I'll send for tea until he is able to see you. His condition is grave for he cannot speak or move his left side, so you mustn't expect conversation. His doctor is working with him to regain his abilities and it's fortunate that he's in Bath where he can be treated and rehabilitated.'

"When tea arrived, Elizabeth had composed herself enough to rejoin the party and eventually Mr. Elliot was allowed to see Sir Walter while his wife waited in the parlour.

"'May I ask how long you and Mr. Elliot have been married?' inquired Anne.

"'It was a recent event and is the source of my greatest happiness for there is no better man in all the world,' she replied with a smile.

"'We wish you all the best for your future happiness together, don't we, Elizabeth?' to which her sister could only respond with a barely audible "yes". Upon their departure, Elizabeth could barely contain her fury.

"'To think I invited her into my own home and embraced her as a friend and confidant and showered her with gifts and opportunities to mingle in superior society. And what should come of it? How does she repay my kindness? She steals my only opportunity for happiness by marrying Mr. Elliot, who was always meant for me. To think that she is destined to be the next Lady Elliot, following in our own dear mother's footsteps. This is untenable. It is an outrage! How shall I bear it? How could he marry her? She has freckles and a protruding tooth. Oh, and that awful clumsy wrist!'

"'Please compose yourself, Elizabeth. You chose an unequal and dangerous companion with an art for pleasing who was worthy only of a distant civility, and you rejected my advising you against it, which allowed her to insinuate herself not only into your life but that of Mr. Elliot.'

"'You must enjoy pointing the finger of blame at me now that you're safely married. Where is your outrage at them? They demean our family name with such a degrading match.'

"Well, the outrage had only just commenced. Mr. Elliot, upon observing the condition of the invalid, realised that he would no longer be able to manage his own affairs. And with the help of Mr. Shepherd, he petitioned the courts to grant him power of attorney over the estate until and unless Sir Walter recovered."

"Now I understand Mr. Shepherd's behaviour when we first arrived," exclaimed Elizabeth. "I was taken by his pride when he showed us the house, almost as if he owned the place, which, of course, he did not, and yet his own daughter was already in line for it."

"Indeed, you are correct, for they took ownership quite soon thereafter when Sir Walter was seized by another stroke within a few months and passed away."

"Poor Miss Elliot. All her years of being at the front of the line on the arm of her father, was left on her own. I must assume her inheritance was generous so that she can live independently?"

"Oh dear, on the contrary, Mrs. Darcy. When Mr. Elliot

discovered the degree of indebtedness of the estate, thanks to Mr. Shepherd, he contrived to pay off the debts and deduct it from any inheritance for Miss Elliot, as it was felt that she was partially responsible for the debt along with her father. Considering the style of living to which she was accustomed, her inheritance could no longer support that lavish standard. She is not impoverished but she was forced to lower her expectations considerably. As we all know, women are often dependent on the size of their dowries to attract the attention of gentlemen of wealth and consequence. Her small fortune, along with her very high expectations of marrying someone of the same social standing, means her opportunities are greatly diminished. Vanity has its price and I'm afraid her reluctance to choose a husband because she was unwilling to sacrifice her exalted role alongside her father, has cost her dearly."

"A very unfair punishment considering women have little control over the purse strings of a husband or a father. She may have enjoyed her luxuries but can hardly be blamed for her father's debts. What a reprehensible decision. It seems like great mischief to heap upon someone who just lost a beloved father," commented Elizabeth.

"Mischief indeed, in my opinion. Knowing Sir William as I do, I'm quite certain his only motivation for marrying Mrs. Clay was to add insult to injury, as I'm sure he has no greater love for her than he did his first wife. And knowing Mrs. Clay, Lady Elliot that is, I have no doubt she connived on her own behalf as well, by convincing Sir William that marrying her would be the most fitting and permanent symbol of disdain for Sir Walter and lower the prospects of his haughty and vain daughter. The man has a very black heart as I well know."

"So, it seems, does his wife, if she was party to the decision."

"Elizabeth was fortunate that her cousin, the Dowager Viscountess Dalrymple, invited her to visit their estate near Dublin. Lady Russell believes she hoped to find a suitable match for her greatly distressed cousin among her own acquaintances, but I've heard no report of such an outcome. They are due to return to Bath quite soon and you will surely meet her for she will be staying with Lady Russell."

"I am greatly obliged to you for your candour, Mrs. Smith. Since we are very likely to meet, your intelligence will help me be better prepared for the occasion."

As Elizabeth made her way home, she marvelled at the perfidy of family connections whom one should hope to be able to trust, and instead betray you for personal gain. While Miss Elliot may be vain and haughty, did she really deserve such betrayal? Based on all that she had learned, Elizabeth could not help but be curious to meet her.

Chapter 9

The evening of the musical soiree at Maple Grove had arrived. Mr. and Mrs. Darcy rode with Georgianna and Kitty, while Colonel Fitzwilliam joined the carriage of the Brandons' and Lady Russell invited Dr. Baldwin to escort her to the event. Maple Grove was an impressive enough estate, although not nearly as grand as Pemberley and the gathering was large, for anyone of social consequence in Bath had been invited. All who gathered were pleased with their surroundings, fashionably attired, socially gratified, and secure in their notion of mutual approbation.

They were greeted effusively by Mrs. Suckling and her husband. A light supper was served, and then all were invited to take a seat before the performances commenced. While Dr. Baldwin knew most of the guests and was greeted cordially by all, he availed himself of the company of Georgianna and Kitty.

"Will you be performing tonight, Miss Darcy?" he asked.

"Oh dear, I dare not for I'm not sure if my level of proficiency would measure up to the other performances and I'm not used to exhibiting before such a large audience. I'm sure my nerves would betray me, and I might forget all that I know for fear of missing a single note. I do hope Mrs. Brandon will play though for she is wonderfully talented and plays with such proficiency and passion. It's as though the composer whispers in her ear and tells her what emotion to express and then her dexterous fingers sublimely translate the music."

"Mrs. Brandon does play very well but, having had the privilege of hearing you, I'm sure you would play beautifully as well, and I am always delighted to listen to one of your performances. Pray consider it tonight and I promise that I shall be your biggest supporter and applaud you over any other performance, if you will."

Georgianna blushed at the compliment but did not commit.

Mrs. Elton approached to introduce her husband and another young couple, Mr. and Mrs. Frank Churchill, to the newly arrived guests.

"How delightful that you could join us. I hope you are pleased with Maple Grove. Everyone who visits is struck by its beauty; the extensive grounds, the grand staircase, all is enchanting. Mr. Darcy, I'm sure you must be pleased with all you see. People of property always appreciate homes of a similar style, is it not true? May I introduce my lord and master, Mr. Elton. Marriage may have transplanted me to another location, but part of me will always be at home here, isn't that right, Mr. E? After growing used to every luxury at Maple

Grove, I had some apprehension about the move to Highbury, but it does have its charms as well, doesn't it, Mr. E?"

"Quite right. The parsonage is particularly well situated and appointed; we lack for nothing and enjoy the goodwill of the most esteemed families in the area," replied Mr. Elton.

Mrs. Elton interjected, "Do let me introduce our very special guests, Mr. Frank Churchill and his lovely wife, Jane, who has always been a personal favourite of mine, haven't you, dear girl? She plays delightfully and her voice is as melodious as that of a nightingale. I'm sure there is no one more welcome in a musical society than dear Jane. Her superior talent when combined with Mr. Churchill's strong baritone is quite exceptional and their duets excite praise wherever they go. I don't claim to have great expertise in such matters as musical performance but my friends say I do and so you may judge for yourselves.

"And here is Mrs. Brandon. How lovely to see you again and how delightful that you could join our party as well. Selina and I had the privilege of hearing her perform when we visited Camden Place to deliver the invitation. What a charming residence in such an elegant location; we were quite taken with it and with Mrs. Brandon. I'm certain her performance will be one of the highlights of the evening.

"We did not have the opportunity to meet the young ladies when we called, but you are most welcome here. I understand Miss Darcy is quite proficient at the pianoforte'. I do hope you plan to exhibit as well, Miss Darcy for I'm sure we will all be delighted if you do.

"Dr. Baldwin, it was so gracious of you to escort Lady

Russell. The party would not have been complete without her presence. So delightful isn't it, Mr. E? You remember Lady Russell. You met her the very year that you proposed to me. It was at a musical event at the Circus. What a happy memory, before Mr. E whisked me off to Highbury, where I met dear Jane. They are just passing through on their way to Weymouth where they first met and became engaged. How romantic, is it not?"

Marianne spoke up. "I'm very glad to see you again, Mrs. Elton. It so happens that Colonel Brandon and I are also on our way to Weymouth in just two days. We expect to be there for a fortnight before returning to Bath for a short visit and then home to Norland Park."

Frank Churchill spoke up. "What a wonderful coincidence. Perhaps our paths will cross. We have a great fondness for Weymouth and will be reuniting with Colonel and Mrs. Campbell and their daughter and her husband. Mrs. Dixon is like a sister to my wife for they were raised together since childhood. You must plan to call on us. We leave tomorrow so shall precede you by a day. It would be a great pleasure to see you there."

As Mrs. Suckling moved about the room, she collected a list of the evening's performers and finally announced the commencement of the event. Each guest was invited to play one piece, but some were encouraged to sign up for two, which the Churchills did at Mrs. Elton's insistence. Elizabeth declined but when pressed, Georgianna complied, with the encouragement of Dr. Baldwin and Darcy. She played admirably with taste and spirit and when she finished, her complexion coloured because, as promised, Dr. Baldwin clapped more loudly than anyone else in the room, followed by her brother, who beamed with pleasure at her performance.

Jane Churchill played splendidly. Her performance, both voice and instrumental, exhibited a natural, unrehearsed refinement that was enchanting. When her husband joined her for the next song, he demonstrated a soaring baritone and perfect knowledge of music, equal to that of his wife. The combination excited the praise of all those in attendance. Clearly, they took as much enjoyment in the music as they did each other.

When Marianne sat down to the instrument, she eschewed the printed musical scores that were available and played from memory. Within the first few notes, she held the audience enthralled, her fingers moving with force and rapidity in a masterful manner that caressed at the beginning and soared to a crescendo at the close. It was as though she had transcended to another place of energy, power, and emotion, and took the audience with her. When she finished, everyone was momentarily silent, and then burst into applause. She was not allowed to quit her seat but was begged to play again and when she did, the audience was equally enraptured.

Colonel Brandon looked on quietly with a slight smile crossing his lips as he observed the response. When Elizabeth inquired if he thought the performance exceptional because of the setting and the size of the audience, he replied, "She plays this way whenever she sits down to the instrument. It's as though all her emotions are exhibited through her fingers and she can do no less than allow them to flow freely. I am blessed each day to have the privilege of hearing her, in private or in public."

As they departed, the Churchills and Brandons exchanged calling cards and promised to meet again in Weymouth and Marianne arranged to visit the Darcys the next morning to play one last time before her departure.

After they returned home and were preparing for bed, Elizabeth commented on how well Georgianna had performed. "I know how difficult it was for her to overcome her shyness performing in such a public setting, but she played beautifully and looked lovely. Weren't you exceptionally proud this evening?"

"Yes, of course. She was delightful, played splendidly, and was greatly admired by all, particularly Dr. Baldwin who seems quite enamoured with her loveliness. Of greater concern is that she seems to welcome his attentions and while I'm sure he's a fine young man, much respected in the community, I can't help but be alarmed for he lacks consequence and connections outside of Bath and has no fortune but that which he earns from his profession. I don't wish to encourage his interest in her or any reciprocal feelings on her part towards him."

"I'm sure it's nothing so serious that you need be concerned, dearest. After all, they were thrown together when we first arrived, and Dr. Baldwin and his brother have been pleasant companions for our sisters and instrumental in making introductions to other acquaintances that have added greatly to the felicity of their time here. I will admit that Georgianna welcomes his attention, but I believe it is the stimulation of exposure to the new ideas and information he presents. She has a much more inquisitive mind than I ever realised. Besides, would it really be so awful if they did form an attachment? We've always discussed that the best marriages are based on love and respect rather than financial gain by either party."

"Elizabeth, I see no reason why a love match can't just as easily result from a propitious introduction to a suitor who is her equal in wealth and consequence. These are not mutually exclusive concepts. As to her newly found interest in science and history, while admirable, it will hardly be of use when she takes on the responsibilities of marriage and raising a family in the future. I must insist on your support in this matter and ask you not to encourage or facilitate the relationship beyond that of casual acquaintances. We must set higher standards for a suitor for Georgianna than any match that Bath has to offer."

Chapter 10

"My dear, I'm pleased to announce we can expect company today for I've received a note from John Willoughby that he's newly arrived in Bath. You remember, I believe, that I mentioned meeting him at my club in London; quite amiable, well informed, and a very fine-looking gentleman in charge of two large estates which he inherited from his recently deceased wife and a beloved aunt. When we discovered our visits in Bath would overlap, he promised to call, and I should like to invite him to dine with us this evening."

"I do remember your writing about him," replied Elizabeth with a raised eyebrow, "and I can't help but wonder if there may be an effort at matchmaking underway?"

Darcy smiled. "Do not judge me harshly, dear wife. He is quite a charming fellow and I'm sure our sisters will be happy to make his acquaintance for he is considered by many to be quite handsome, and he is an eligible man of good fortune. You mustn't hold that against him."

"It may well be that he is wealthy, but do you think, my dear, that he is also a man of good character?" she teased.

"Let us not make a rush to judgement; after all, we judged each other rather harshly when we first met," replied Darcy.

"Very true, very true, and, as fate would have it, your character was much to be esteemed as I later learned, and your opinion of me improved with time as well. One must be cautious about first impressions and passing judgement on a new acquaintance too quickly. I remember you wrote that he was recently widowed. Such a sad business to lose his wife and child at birth."

"Indeed, very sad. He'd just removed the crepe from his hat and set his period of mourning aside when we met."

When Mr. Willoughby arrived that evening, he entered the room with a graceful elegance and relaxed charm. Without putting on airs, he engaged the family with cordiality and friendliness that was disarming. They spoke of Bath and its attractions, especially for first-time visitors and he mentioned that it had been several years since his last visit.

To the young ladies he was a model of masculine perfection, but Kitty and Georgianna were also struck by his playful conversation. He inquired about their visit including where they had been, what they had done, and whom they had met. He seemed to take unabashed pleasure in their responses. Upon learning they had frequented the Upper Assembly he professed his own great love of music and dancing. Georgianna kept her gaze lowered but Kitty's eyes lit up with pleasure at his attentions.

The evening included performances at the pianoforte by

Georgianna at Mr. Willoughby's request. She agreed to play but not to sing and sat down to the instrument. She completed the first selection with an accomplished precision and then turned to another song book for the second. To her surprise, Willoughby walked over to join her and began singing the verse to accompany her play. He had an assured voice and tone and the effect was charming. At first startled by the move, Georgianna soon relaxed and the impression they made was admired by all. They continued through a third performance before stopping. Everyone commented on the delightful voice of Willoughby and the accomplishment of Georgianna. He of course dismissed the compliments of his own talents and directed all to the performance of the lady. The evening closed with promises of exploring the gardens the next day and a visit to the Upper Assembly that evening.

The next afternoon Willoughby joined them for the walking tour and showed equal attention to both the young ladies. Georgianna's usual shyness was on display, but Kitty eagerly responded to all his attentions, to the amusement of Elizabeth and chagrin of Darcy. Later that day, Elizabeth overheard Kitty and Georgianna talking about their new acquaintance.

"Oh, Georgie, is he not uncommonly handsome and accomplished? Such a charming voice and gentlemanly manners. Were you not thrilled when he joined you to sing last evening? I was thankful that I don't play for it allowed me to just gaze at him. He moves with such grace and speaks so amiably about any manner of topics and he loves dancing! What greater felicity is there than finding a handsome man who loves to dance? I'm sure he'll wish to invite you first at the Assembly, but I hope he dances with me next for I know I would float across the dance floor with him as my partner."

"I quite agree Mr. Willoughby is an exceedingly handsome and charming man and he sings very well. I was discomposed when he first joined me, but he made it seem easy once the song was underway. He is very open and engaging but I find it difficult to respond to his courtesies and conversation. I blush every time he speaks to me and cannot overcome my shyness."

"Stay shy then as long as it pleases you, dear Georgie, and I will do the talking for both of us," laughed Kitty.

That evening at the Assembly Hall, Willoughby did invite Georgianna to dance first and escorted her to join the other couples. Mr. Baldwin had recently arrived and took Kitty out to the floor.

"With whom is Miss Darcy dancing?" he inquired. "I don't believe I've seen the gentleman before."

"He is an acquaintance of her brother and has just arrived in Bath. He is a widower, which is a very regrettable state I am sure, but despite his loss, he is very amiable and charming. We met him last evening for the first time and he performed with Georgianna who played while he sang. He has a marvellous voice. Everyone is quite taken with him."

"I hope my brother arrives soon, so he doesn't engage her for all of the dances."

"Oh no, he's promised the next dance to me," Kitty replied with a confident smile.

Dr. Baldwin did arrive shortly thereafter and greeted Mr. and Mrs. Darcy. They exchanged pleasantries and Elizabeth could not help but notice his gaze followed Georgianna almost exclusively. When the dance concluded and the partners left the floor, Willoughby was introduced by Georgianna, and a pleasant exchange followed. He took a good deal of interest in the history of Bath and the treatments that Dr. Baldwin provided to his patients.

When the music commenced again, Willoughby led Kitty to the dance floor and Dr. Baldwin escorted Georgianna. Here again Elizabeth observed the relaxed manner and easy conversation between the two. Georgianna neither blushed nor looked away from his addresses but seemed to engage him with confidence.

Kitty was glowing on the arm of her partner as the ensemble of dancers followed the prescribed steps of a country dance. When the break came and they transitioned to the other room, she made every effort to stay near Willoughby and engage him in conversation.

Elizabeth realised that while Darcy had hopes that Georgianna would be smitten, it appeared that Kitty was the one most eager for Mr. Willoughby's attentions. He had the breeding of a gentleman, he was engaging, well read, with opinions that confirmed good judgement, and was charmingly open in conversation. His ease with people was so unguarded that she wondered if he was used to having things his way without a great deal of effort. She wondered also about the wont of any evidence of melancholia for his lost wife and child.

When she mentioned Willoughby's seeming lack of sadness or reserve after only a year of bereavement, Darcy came to his defence. "A cheerful disposition does not necessarily reflect a lack of inner suffering. You mustn't judge him because he is amiable and engaging in company, for he may very well choose to keep such feelings of remorse to himself. And why should he not put himself forward in company? He is a man of wealth and position and has every right to get on with his life and seek new entertainments and companions. I'm surprised at your concern, my dear. I should think you would embrace a man of consequence in our midst and the possibility of a love match for my sister, especially one that would be such a desirable alliance of equals."

"Please don't misunderstand my concern. If your sister admires and esteems Mr. Willoughby above all others and wishes for a match, she has my full support and I would rejoice for her as much as you, but you can't deny that we know very little of him and can't assume that just because he is a man of wealth that he is a man of good character."

"Really, my dear, please do not dispute me on this matter. You are, perhaps, naïve having grown up in a small community, and should leave it to me as a man of the world to judge whether his character is worthy, for I have far more experience than you. I have always held the best interests of my sister close to my heart, but it is incumbent on me to find her a suitable match. Of course, her happiness is and always has been my utmost concern, and I would never do anything to put it at risk. I ask for your indulgence."

Elizabeth was greatly vexed by the discussion. It was the first time since they had married that there had been any sort of disagreement between them. There was an arrogance to his demeanour and a dismissiveness of her feelings that she hadn't encountered since they first met. She had learned to rely on teasing to subdue his pride and bring an end to any quarrelling between them, which occurred rarely anyway. There was a haughtiness in his manner at times, but they were always able to reach an accord thanks to her good humour and gentle prodding.

This was not a matter that could be teased away. He was steadfast in his opinion and sense of duty to secure a desirable match for his sister, especially having escaped the debacle of Georgianna falling under the influence of Mr. Wickham and almost eloping with him at a tender age. That her own sister, Lydia, had fallen into that same trap and eloped with Wickham was a painful reminder to them of the vagaries of fortune that can lead to unplanned consequences from capricious choices. Elizabeth could not blame him for being protective of his sister.

Why could she not overcome her own uneasiness with Mr. Willoughby? She had attempted to express her condolences for the loss of his wife and child the evening they met. He responded with sombre and gracious acceptance but quickly moved on to more convivial conversation. She wondered how Darcy would have responded if her pregnancy had developed further and she had gone into labour and died along with her baby. She was sure his bereavement would have been prolonged and emotionally devastating. Perhaps Willoughby's attachment to his wife hadn't been as strong. But was it fair to make comparisons? Was she rushing to judgement? Disabused that her husband had been dismissive of her concerns?

Annoyed with his condescension? Was she importuned because of her own recent loss?

Her only avenue for expression was to write to Jane and share her concerns and grievances knowing full well that Jane, who could only see the good in everyone, would counsel her to be patient with her husband and open to the merits of the potential suitor. Still, there would be some relief in composing the letter and sharing her feelings, so she took out pen and paper from her writing desk and began.

My Dearest Jane,

It grieves me to write to you when I am in such a state of perturbation, but it is the only way to excise the demons of frustration and anger that disturb my tranquillity. For the first time since we married, my husband and I are at odds about the marriage prospects of dear Georgianna, and we have reached a stage of quarrelling over a suitor he has brought into our midst for whom I see no evidence of attachment on the part of his sister. Instead, his concern is growing that she is enamoured with a local doctor from a highly respected family, whilst I am concerned about the character of the gentleman he favours, of whom we know very little aside from the fact that he is very wealthy and recently widowed. They met at his men's club during a recent business trip to London and discovered that they both would be visiting Bath at the same time.

Mr. John Willoughby is a very well looking gentleman, charming, worldly, genteel, but he has such an easy way about him that draws the admiration of others and yet I find him rather artful with his impeccable manners and practiced graces, who shows no signs of mourning the loss of his wife and baby during childbirth. I know I should not be so judgmental but there it is, I am mistrustful. Georgianna is pleasant and courteous towards him but doesn't appear comfortable with his attention while Kitty, on the other hand, seems besotted. As to the local doctor, he is much admired for his focus on providing remedies for his patients based on his extensive knowledge of the mineral hot springs that draw people from many locales to seek help for their maladies, and he has been very effective in treating them. He provided care to the former resident of Camden Place who was felled by a stroke that partially paralysed the poor baronet and eventually he passed away, but another patient that I know has been helped immeasurably with her mobility for a rheumatic condition by him.

Georgianna is a revelation when in Dr. Baldwin's presence and takes a great deal of interest in the scientific studies he conducts while developing remedies for his patients. He is the only gentleman with whom she seems genuinely at ease and comfortable and they engage endlessly in conversation about shared interests in his successful treatments. His family is highly esteemed in the area but, unfortunately, he is a second son with no inheritance and earns a living with his medical practice which causes my dear husband, who considers him unworthy, no end of concern that an attachment may be forming.

I'm afraid we find ourselves at odds with one another even though I am in no way promoting an attachment to the one gentleman but have wariness of the other. You and I were blessed to marry men for whom we had true affection, and I can only wish such felicity for both of our sisters and that they be free to choose for themselves. To be honest, even if Kitty were the object of Mr. Willoughby's attention, I would still have misgivings and uncertainty about his character.

I can almost predict how you will respond, dearest Jane; that I should be patient with my husband and not prejudge the suitor he brought into our midst, but I find myself ill at ease with the entire situation, most especially the rift with my beloved husband. I will do my best to be patient and avoid being judgmental but welcome your guidance as my most trusted friend.

Please do give my very best regards to your husband and kiss little Amy for me.

Your loving sister,

Lizzy D

Chapter 11

The agitation of mind that already afflicted Elizabeth was further heightened a few days later when she received a letter from her sister, Mary. She hoped it might be a letter from Jane with news of her family and advice for herself as she'd written recently but had heard nothing back. She thought this might be an application for more assistance to the parsonage as Mary was never shy about any requests made in the name of charity but, instead, the application took a different form.

Dearest Lizzy,

I write to share the best possible news, that Mr. Wink and I are expecting our first child. I've missed my monthly courses recently and the doctor has confirmed that I am with child. You can imagine the excitement and delight that we are experiencing. Mama and Papa have been informed already and now I write to share the wonderful news with my sisters so

you can partake in our joy. I desired to share the happy tidings
as well as to beg a favour.

I'm sure you'll recall the day that we explored the storage
room at Pemberley to identify items to donate to the annual
charity event that Mr. Wink organises. There were baby
furnishings that you declined to give away at the time as I am
sure you were thinking to put them aside for use by your own
child someday. While I am exceedingly sorry for your recent
loss, it appears you have no immediate need for those items
while I have an imminent need. I hope and pray that your
circumstances will change someday soon, and you will have
your own happy news to share, if it is God's will, but I must
beg your indulgence in this matter. Afterall, you can easily
afford new furniture when your time arrives, but the
circumstances at the parsonage require us to live within more
limited means. Remember, it is in giving that we receive, and
perhaps God will grant your wish for a child more quickly if
you give up your attachment to those items that we will need
very soon.

I hope that your stay in Bath has refreshed your spirits and
that our sister, Kitty, has been a model of propriety. A
woman's virtue, once lost, can never be recovered. May God
bless you and keep you. Give my regards to Kitty and remind
her of my admonition. I remain your devoted sister,

Mary W

Elizabeth sat stricken and her eyes welled with tears. While
she wished her sister well and tried to rejoice in Mary's news,
she could not help but feel despondent over her own situation,

for despite having everything in the world from a loving and generous husband to a rich and prosperous life, she was missing her true heart's desire, a child to love, and an heir for Pemberley.

Right at that moment, the parlour door opened, and Dr. Baldwin was announced. Seeing the look on her face, he immediately approached her and inquired what could possibly be wrong.

"I do hope my visit doesn't importune you. I stopped by to call on the Misses Darcy and Bennet but find you indisposed. Is there anything I can do to help? Shall I call for your husband? How may I be of service? I see you have a letter in your lap. Did you receive bad news?"

Elizabeth dabbed her tears and forced herself to smile. "On the contrary, it is very good news. I've just learned my younger sister, Mary, is expecting a child." With that, her lip quivered, and the tears streamed again. "I don't know what's come over me for this is a joyful announcement."

Dr. Baldwin, with a look of concern, pulled a chair closer to sit near her. "I don't mean to be indelicate, but I did learn from Miss Darcy that you recently experienced a loss of your own and that is why you came to Bath. It is quite understandable that your response to this news would cause you some amount of pain, despite your happiness for your sister."

"It is true. I have tried to leave the pain of loss behind, but it follows me still. I was so happy and hopeful before, and now I feel so inadequate; that I have somehow failed my husband. He has been so loving and supportive throughout this ordeal, but I can't seem to manage my feelings. Producing an heir is my heart's desire and I fear it may not happen. The doctor recommended we wait awhile before trying again, but I cannot see how that will help or relieve my despondency. My sister has asked to use the nursery furnishings from when Georgianna was a baby, and I treasure those items because, when I discovered them stored away, they became the symbol of promise for a child in our future. I had such plans to bring them out and restore them when our baby was due. Now I have no need of them, and she does. It would be selfish to deny her request, but it feels like I would be giving up hope by giving them away and my heart feels broken at the thought of it. I don't know how I shall manage to overcome this despondency."

"Although my medical practice doesn't usually include the birthing of babies, do you mind if I ask you a few questions?"

"You've been very kind. Of course, you may ask what you like."

"Are your monthly courses regular and do you experience much pain when they occur?"

"Yes, they are quite regular, and I only occasionally experience discomfort. Why do you ask?"

"I know of some women who experience extreme pain whenever they occur and have tried to provide relief for their condition through medication and relaxation in the baths. It seems to be an effective remedy, and it occurs to me that perhaps you would benefit from this as well. Since you don't experience intense pain, the medicinal side may not be necessary, but the relaxation provided by the healing waters would benefit you. May I ask how far into your pregnancy you were and what happened during it?"

"I had missed two of my monthly courses and the doctor confirmed it a few weeks later. We were so excited by the news but shortly thereafter I began spotting and was ordered to rest in bed. Despite my best efforts, the loss came within a few more days and I was so devastated. The doctor assured me that it was not uncommon for a first pregnancy and that I should have no trouble in the future."

Dr. Baldwin nodded gravely. "Did you experience any swelling of your limbs during the time?" he asked.

"No, none whatever. I seemed perfectly healthy until the signs showed otherwise."

"That is very good news. I agree with your doctor that there should be no impediment to a healthy pregnancy and your ability to give birth. May I make a recommendation?"

"Yes, of course; I shall gladly listen to any advice you have."

"When your next course begins, I'd like you to visit the baths and immerse yourself for thirty minutes every day for two weeks. We have private areas with bathtubs that can be filled from the hot springs and later drained and scrubbed. You need not fear any infection from the use. Your troubled mind needs relief and I believe the relaxation will help both body and spirit. You must promise to spend the thirty minutes focusing on those things which bring you joy and avoid thoughts that depress you. I will make all the arrangements for your comfort and privacy if you agree to the plan."

"I gratefully accept your offer, Dr. Baldwin," replied Elizabeth with relief. "You are so very kind and understanding; I thank you for your concern and advice. I already feel partially recovered just to be able to share my feelings," she replied with a smile.

With that, the sound of voices was heard, and Kitty and Georgianna entered carrying parcels from their latest shopping expedition. They expressed their surprise and delight at finding Dr. Baldwin there.

"I came to invite you to visit my laboratory in two weeks' time as I'm expecting delivery of a new microscope and thought you might be interested in seeing it. I know that may sound rather dull, but I assure you that it is quite remarkable to view a drop of pond water, a blade of grass, or the wing of a fly through the device."

"I would be very excited to see what you describe and I'm sure my brother would support any effort to improve my learning. I shall ask him right away," enthused Georgianna. The friends continued discussing the plan until Dr. Baldwin departed with a special bow and nod to Elizabeth.

Elizabeth shared the news from Mary while dining that evening and great delight was expressed by all, but Darcy kept a close eye on his wife, aware of her emotional state and the impact the news may have had. When Mr. Willoughby came by to escort Georgianna and Kitty to the theatre, he was relieved to have time alone with her. He worried that all the social engagements were taking a toll on her for she was used to a much quieter existence at Pemberley and had no need of the entertainments that so enticed the young ladies. Colonel

Fitzwilliam had travelled to Bristol on business, and he was grateful to have someone else who was trustworthy to take their sisters out in society.

"How was your day, Elizabeth? How did you take the news from Mary? I fear it may have distressed you, especially after I read her letter. What do you think of her request? You know that I would be happy to purchase anything they need to prepare for the birth of their child and there is no need to trouble yourself, especially if it disturbs your tranquillity."

Elizabeth smiled sadly. "I can have no reserve on this subject with you, my dearest. The news did cause me a temporary perturbation, stirring up regret and sadness to be sure. In truth, my emotions overtook me, and I was quite beside myself when a visitor arrived. It was Dr. Baldwin. He was so kind and understanding that I could not contain my wretchedness at the news, despite my happiness for my sister. He was most professional in his demeanour and assured me that he had prior knowledge of my loss, because Georgianna had taken him into her confidence by explaining the motivation for our trip to Bath."

"Georgianna should have shown more discretion than to reveal private family matters to a casual acquaintance. I shall speak to her about this."

"I'm sure she meant no harm, especially considering that he is a doctor. He was very sympathetic and made inquiries about my condition during my pregnancy. Indeed, he was very professional and reassured me about the likelihood of success in the future. He even made a specific recommendation that I visit the baths daily for two weeks when my monthly course begins. He believes the experience will allow my body to relax and my mind to find peace with the restorative powers of the water."

"I'm glad that someone was here to console you when the letter arrived. Dr. Baldwin seems like a very honourable gentleman, and he is quite knowledgeable and experienced despite his youth. It was kind of him to offer you solace and a possible remedy; if you wish to avail yourself of his services, you have my blessing, especially if it will help to restore your tranquillity. Nevertheless, I don't approve of Georgianna discussing such intimate matters with a new acquaintance."

"Did you by chance share the story of our loss with Mr. Willoughby when you first met him?"

"Certainly not! I am by nature very reserved, as you know. Well, perhaps I did mention it but only as a means of consoling him for his own loss as it seemed the kind thing to do. Ordinarily I would never share news of our disappointment with a new acquaintance."

Her eyes welled up as she said, "I'm so sorry to have disappointed you."

"No, my love, no. You mustn't blame yourself. It couldn't be helped, and we both share the sense of loss. I wish only for your happiness and contentment. Please do just as Dr. Baldwin suggested and make every effort you can to restore your tranquillity."

"I think it behooves you to accept that the girls and I consider Dr. Baldwin to be a friend, not a mere acquaintance, and I'm sure there can be no harm in that."

"You're quite right. I must admit I was rather amused at the news of an invitation to visit his laboratory and the enthusiasm of my sister to look through a microscope. Despite my misgivings of a possible attachment, I've decided to join them on the visit, for I'm rather curious myself. My own education wasn't focused on the sciences to any great extent, but we do live in a modern world and should be open to adapting to new things."

"Georgianna is a revelation these days," said Elizabeth. "Young ladies are raised to curtsy properly, dance gracefully, cover screens, read aloud, play an instrument, and other useful employments. Who would have supposed that her natural curiosity would be directed to history and science, and yet, she hangs on every word spoken by Dr. Baldwin, and she shares that which she has learned so enthusiastically? Where there is no opportunity for a woman to apply her natural interests to everyday life, there is no reason for them to be taught. It seems we are meant for adornment alone rather than making use of our minds."

"My dear Elizabeth, you know the great respect I have for your excellent mind and how you apply yourself. In fact, I depend upon it, yet I cannot deny that few women ever have an opportunity in education beyond the usual social graces; perhaps the world would be better off if they did. Men have the say of it, although many of them fail to apply themselves when given the opportunity. My unfortunate brother-in-law, Wickham, is a prime example of a wasted mind and wasted life."

"I cannot argue with you on that point but can only add that his choice in a wife aptly matched his own inclinations. Neither he nor Lydia have ever exercised restraint or applied themselves to practical matters in life, more's the pity."

Chapter 12

Elizabeth soon began her daily visits to the baths each morning and occasionally crossed paths with Mrs. Smith who went for treatments three days a week. Although their therapies were strikingly different, for Mrs. Smith's exercises were based on specific activities and she was lifted into the hot springs by use of a bath chair, while Elizabeth's therapy was based on simple relaxation in a private tub, they would sometimes visit Lady Russell when they were done. One day they came to call and discovered there was already another visitor, Mrs. Anne Wentworth, newly arrived in Bath with her husband. The ladies engaged in an extended conversation and Anne was eager to hear about Elizabeth's comfort and felicity while staying at Camden Place.

"Do the accommodations suit your tastes and is the location to your liking?" she asked. "My father, Sir Walter Elliot, took great pride in the furnishings and appointments when he moved to Bath. He was dotingly fond of the finest particulars and no detail was too small for his notice."

"We are very happy with the accommodations, although we did store a few of the mirrors which seemed to be everywhere, and we arranged to bring in a pianoforte' which has made for pleasant evenings of entertainment," replied Elizabeth. "The location is perfectly convenient, and we enjoy the access to shops and gardens. My husband and I travelled here with our younger sisters, Miss Darcy, and Miss Bennet, and they have been particularly fond of the entertainments Bath offers as well as the acquaintances they have made. We were especially grateful to Mr. Shepherd for his early introductions to Lady Russell and Dr. Baldwin, which have added greatly to the felicity of our stay."

Anne smiled and nodded but a look passed between her and Lady Russell before she commented that she was happy that Mr. Shepherd had been of service and delighted that the acquaintance had developed into friendships with two of the people most dear to her, Lady Russell and Mrs. Smith. Inquiries were made about lengths of stay, amusements to be pursued, and favourite haunts. The pending arrival of her sister, Miss Elliot, was discussed and Elizabeth took the opportunity to express her condolences for the loss of their father and the desire to entertain them all at Camden Place after Miss Elliot arrived, unless a visit would cause them unnecessary distress. Anne assured her she was quite certain a visit to their former home would be most welcomed by herself and her sister.

The discussion turned to Dr. Baldwin and his medical

practice, and inquiries were made about Elizabeth's daily visits to the baths and how she was enjoying the experience. All agreed that Dr. Baldwin's remedies seemed to greatly benefit those who came under his care and Mrs. Smith's recovery of her mobility and relief from her rheumatic condition was a prime example of the efficacy of his therapies. His gracious introduction to Bath, which included giving them a tour of the city soon after their arrival, his enthusiasm for visiting the Assembly Hall, and abilities as a dance partner all added to the general approbation of his good character. Mrs. Wentworth expressed her hopes of introducing the Darcys to Captain Wentworth very soon, and that brought the engagement to a close.

"Mrs. Wentworth is a delightful acquaintance," declared Elizabeth to her husband that evening. "I have not met Captain Wentworth yet, but I am sure we will like him, if his wife is any example of his good character. She is charming, well informed, amusing, and infinitely good company. I've invited them for an evening here after Miss Elliot's arrival, but hope we shall meet them socially much sooner for I am curious to make his acquaintance. I expect we will meet Admiral Croft and his wife as well, for I understand they are just arrived from Kellynch Hall. The end of the war has allowed them both to settle after so many years at sea. What a coincidence that they served together, and that Captain Wentworth would end up married to the baronet's daughter while his sister, the admiral's wife, occupies the home of Sir Walter's former seat. Who could predict such a connection?"

"Surely it is a quirk of fate and yet so, perhaps, are we my dear. Fate brought us together because we were meant for each other," replied Darcy with a smile.

Kitty and Georgianna returned from an outing with Mr. Willoughby, declaring a plan to attend a concert that evening, as he had arranged to purchase tickets for them all. They arrived early and stationed themselves near a fireplace in the octagon room to await entrance to the concert hall. Willoughby directed his attentions to the young ladies and was engaging them in conversation about the musical agenda. Kitty seemed to hang on his every word and made every effort to be amiable and engaging while Georgianna nodded politely to his commentary while her eyes wandered the room until they suddenly brightened when she saw Dr. Baldwin enter. Upon seeing him, Georgianna spoke up and invited him to join their conversation and it did not go unobserved by her brother and his wife, that her complexion flushed, and her manner became more animated as they spoke. Willoughby was polite and engaging towards the doctor but continued to direct most of his addresses towards Georgianna, who seemed distracted by trying to listen to the one conversation while trying to continue another with Dr. Baldwin.

Darcy could not help but notice the contrast and felt frustration that his careful planning was being thwarted by the arrival of the doctor. Lizzy could not help but notice her husband's reaction and only hoped that he would learn to accept the natural course of affection that seemed to be developing between Dr. Baldwin and Georgianna.

Within a few moments the doors were opened, and everyone entered the room to claim seats and review the concert bill. The Darcys entered first followed by Willoughby, who stationed himself between Kitty and Georgianna, leaving the doctor at the end of the bench. Kitty directed much of her attention to Willoughby although she made some effort at polite conversation with Dr. Baldwin, inquiring after his brother, and asking if he was expected to be in attendance that evening. Dr. Baldwin shared that his brother, Thomas, was not fond of concerts and preferred the excitement and activities of the Upper Assembly with the focus on dancing. To this Kitty acknowledged a similar inclination before turning her attentions once more to Willoughby.

When the intermission came and a quest for tea was pursued, Elizabeth noticed a tall, very well-looking man with stately bearing across the room. To her surprise, he was joined by none other than Anne Wentworth. Delighted at the opportunity to make his acquaintance, she took her husband's arm and approached them with an amiable greeting.

"Mrs. Wentworth. What a happy surprise to make your acquaintance twice in one day! May I introduce my husband, Mr. Darcy?" Cordialities were exchanged between the two couples, the concert program was discussed, the quality of the orchestra approved, and expressions of delight exchanged at the unexpected meeting. Darcy reiterated his wife's earlier invitation to receive them at Camden Place when Miss Elliot returned, and a discussion ensued about the timetable for her arrival and where she had been staying in Ireland.

The Darcys had just rejoined their party and shared the news about the new acquaintance to the general approbation of all. Georgianna was engaged in conversation with Dr.

Baldwin, when the announcement that the orchestra was to commence playing came. This time she managed to hold back briefly while Elizabeth struck up a discussion with Mr. Willoughby about the second half of the program, so that when they re-entered the hall, she was able to place herself next to her friend when they were seated again. It may be implied that Georgianna enjoyed the second half of the concert a good deal more than she had the first, while Kitty cared very little about the concert but enjoyed herself immensely whenever Mr. Willoughby directed his conversation to her.

Later that evening Darcy expressed his consternation over the way that Dr. Baldwin availed himself of Georgianna's attentions at the expense of Willoughby's efforts to converse with her.

"I don't understand how she can ignore the attentions of a handsome, charming, and wealthy gentleman of consequence and hang on every word uttered by a local country doctor. It's unbecoming. She should know her place in the world and not invite the attentions of someone so wholly beneath her."

"I seem to recollect that you had a similar view of me when first we met; that I was beneath you in consequence as was my sister, Jane, beneath Mr. Bingley. In fact, you long struggled against your feelings before revealing them the first time you asked me to be your wife."

"That was different. I was mistaken. I had only to realise my arrogance had destroyed any opportunity of happiness with you to regret it. I was humbled by your rejection and came to love you even more and it is the blessing of my existence that you finally accepted me."

"Don't you wish for Georgianna's happiness as well? Would you pressure her to accept someone she doesn't love just because he's a man of wealth and consequence? And what do we know of his character? We've only just become acquainted with him, but it causes me some uneasiness that he seems so little distressed by the loss of his family and eager to attach himself to someone else after only a year of mourning. I would be distressed indeed at the thought that you would be so lacking in emotion if something happened to me."

"Of course, I wish for her happiness! How can you doubt it? My only wish is for her to be as happily married as we are. I merely hope she sets her sights higher. Is that so wrong?"

It was the first real argument since they married that Elizabeth had not tried to tease him into a better humour, nor was she inclined to do so.

Chapter 13

The following week, Elizabeth received a note from Mrs. Brandon announcing their return from Weymouth and a desire to call on her at Camden Place, to which she replied with an invitation to join her the next afternoon for tea. She was eager to see her new friend and hear news of their travels and whether they had contacted the Churchills during their stay.

Marianne arrived at the appointed time and they were soon engrossed in conversation. Weymouth had been a delightful place to visit, they had seen the Churchills almost daily and participated in as many musical interludes as they could conspire to arrange.

"It was such a relief to find the Churchills such an amiable couple, and the Campbells and Dixons were superior company. I was thankful to find such a charming group of people, despite, if I may say it, the source of the introduction. I believe that Mrs. Elton's claim on the affections of Jane Churchill, are hardly reciprocated but merely tolerated.

"I understand that when Jane came to Highbury to visit her relatives, the newly married Mrs. Elton had just arrived and sought to ingratiate herself with Jane by promoting a future role as a governess to one of her acquaintances. No one knew at the time that Jane was secretly engaged to Mr. Churchill. In fact, everyone in the community thought that he was destined to marry a handsome, clever, and rich young woman named Emma Woodhouse, who was intimately acquainted with Mr. Churchill's father, Mr. Weston, and his new wife; for Mrs. Weston had once been the governess of Miss Woodhouse and they were very close. Mr. Weston was a widower who adopted out his young son to the Churchills after his wife passed away but always stayed in contact with his natural son.

"Although Jane's prospects in life were limited and despite the affection that developed between her and Mr. Churchill when they first met in Weymouth, it seemed that a future together was doomed by the demands and dependency of his adoptive mother. Her death freed him to marry the object of his affection and enjoy the felicity they do now."

"Not all of one's connections in life are as convivial as others," admitted Elizabeth, "but sometimes one must make do out of courtesy. I celebrate such an agreeable outcome for them; to marry for love is indeed a blessing."

"Frankly, I believe that to be taken under the wing of an overly pert and familiar woman with an inflated sense of her own importance is too much to be endured, but they are reconciled to tolerate her condescension because of their family connections in Highbury.

"I am thankful for the insistence of Mrs. Elton that the

Churchills visit Bath after she heard they would be travelling to Weymouth. Their performance at the musical soiree was a delight and we were happy to become better acquainted with them in a place where our mutual interest in music was allowed to flourish. Our felicity was even greater because my husband and Colonel Campbell discovered many shared interests, so it made for a most compatible arrangement. We stayed almost a week longer than we originally planned."

"Well then, it is fortuitous that Bath was the destination that brought all of us together and that the rendezvous in Weymouth was so amiable," replied Elizabeth. "I'm sure I would have enjoyed the performances of such a talented group. I would invite you to take up your morning visits to play our instrument, but my mornings have been taken up by visits to the baths at the recommendation of Dr. Baldwin. However, you are more than welcome to play in the afternoons."

"I thank you kindly for the offer, but we will only be in town for a few days and I believe my desire to perform has been quite satiated during our travels. However, I do hope to see you frequently while we are here and look forward to hearing Miss Darcy perform again. I don't wish to importune you, but may I ask about the treatment recommended by Dr. Baldwin? I hope you are not indisposed with illness or discomfort."

"Only discomfort of the mind," replied Elizabeth. "You see I suffered a loss during an early stage of pregnancy which caused me great distress. My husband thought an extended stay in Bath would provide a distraction and lift my spirits, which is how we came to be here this season. I still find myself troubled and concerned about my ability to give birth, which came to the attention of Dr. Baldwin. He believes that mind and body are intimately connected and suggested that relief from the stress of the loss could be remedied by daily relaxation. I find it does have a transformative effect and I've continued beyond the two weeks that he first recommended, as I am rather enjoying it and look forward to the visits."

"Dr. Baldwin seems like such a treasure to the community. Everyone seems to admire him," said Marianne.

"He is indeed. I only wish my husband admired him more. Georgianna and Dr. Baldwin seem very enamoured with each other, but my husband has objections about his wealth and connections. He is a second son and will not inherit an estate, so he studies the sciences and practices medicine which my husband considers beneath his sister's station in life. He has another more prosperous candidate in mind whom I must admit is handsome and charming, but most important to my husband, he is wealthy with more than one estate."

"Why is it that wealth and connections outweigh natural affection when it comes to matrimonial choices? I too once formed an attachment to someone and suffered disappointment when he chose another for the size of her fortune and to please his aunt, but I no longer regret it because it led me to my dear Colonel Brandon who is far more deserving of love and affection than he ever was. Well, I must be off, but I do so hope the therapy helps renew your confidence and brings you your heart's desire. I am sure you cannot help but succeed and I wish you well. We leave in a few days, but I promise to call again soon."

~~*~*

"Dearest, I've just received a letter from Sir Thomas Bertram that he will be travelling from Bristol to Bath on his way home to his estate in Northampton and wishes to pay a call. You'll recollect that my solicitor, John Varley, arranged the sale of our property in Antigua to him. He made the acquaintance of my cousin, Colonel Fitzwilliam, who has been in Bristol this past week and it appears that both will be arriving in Bath next week."

"I believe we shall have to add to our guest list then," replied Elizabeth. "Since we already plan a party for the Wentworths and Miss Elliot to visit Camden Place, we shall have to expand to include them. I do hope the Brandons will still be in town, and I plan to invite Lady Russell and Dr. Baldwin. Of course, we must include Mr. Willoughby if he remains in Bath. We shall have a musical night of it with all those guests in attendance. From what I've heard of Miss Elliot, having a baronet in our company will quite put her at ease that she is in superior society."

"Must we invite Dr. Baldwin? I fear he will monopolise Georgianna."

"Of course, we must. He is a great favourite of our guests and cared for Mrs. Wentworth's and Miss Elliott's father when he was stricken and he's a dear friend of Lady Elliott's as well. Besides, Georgianna would be very disappointed if he wasn't invited."

"Aye, and your sister will be all too happy for

Willoughby's attentions. Would that the opposite was true. Nevertheless, we shall fix on a date once we ascertain the schedules of our guests," replied Darcy.

"I wonder if Dr. Baldwin's new microscope has arrived yet. I believe we are all quite curious to visit his laboratory. I understand it is on the grounds of his father's estate, Holbourn, rather than at his offices in town. His brother, Thomas, also lives on the estate and pursues his interests in raising horses and terriers. I'm told by Georgianna that their father has a great interest in architecture and was instrumental in the design of Pultney Street as well as a modest extension of Sydney Place. I suppose Dr. Baldwin's multi-faceted interests must be the consequence of exposure to his father's."

"Georgianna seems to know quite a lot about that family. I must say it is unusual for a gentleman of property to be involved in civic development," replied Darcy. "I wonder that he had the time and inclination to pursue such interests. However, I do admire the attention to design and detail by the architects of Bath; it is a beautiful city and I suppose it is for the best that his youngest son has found his place in the world since he can't rely on an inheritance."

"Quite right, dearest; Dr. Baldwin is such an asset to the community and greatly admired."

"Admired by my sister in particular I'm afraid, much to my chagrin."

Later that day Elizabeth met Lady Russell and Mrs. Wentworth for tea at the Pump Room when they were joined by Captain Wentworth, his sister, and her husband, Admiral Croft. She was captivated by Mrs. Croft's stories of travelling with her husband and visiting many ports of call. Never had she encountered a woman so adventurous as to travel onboard a ship; indeed, she didn't even know it was possible for wives to travel with their husbands that way. Clearly there was great warmth and openness shared by this group who seemed to take great delight in each other's company and were very welcoming to her. On returning home she suggested to her husband that they include the Crofts in the upcoming party.

"I'm sure they will be very amiable guests whom you will greatly enjoy. And I care not that Miss Elliot might look down on the Crofts as the 'renters' of her former home. Lady Russell confided to me that when they first moved to Bath, Miss Elliot had expressed reluctance to introduce them to her cousin, the Dowager Viscountess Dalrymple, lest they be an acquaintance of whom she might not approve. Can you imagine? She was said to state that the Crofts should be left to find their own level in society. I dare say I found them to be perfectly charming people and I am eager for you to meet them."

"Well surely if we can invite a baronet, we can invite an admiral?" replied Darcy.

As they spoke, a note arrived from Dr. Baldwin inviting them to visit his laboratory two days hence. "Well, here is our answer to the question of the whereabouts of the microscope. Apparently, it has just arrived, and we shall see it soon," said Elizabeth.

Georgianna greeted the invitation with supreme delight and immediately enlisted Kitty to go shopping for ribbons to adorn her new bonnet. While Kitty was less enthused about visiting a laboratory, she did express her hope that Thomas Baldwin would be there because he was so amiable, and she hoped she could meet some of his dogs.

Chapter 14

The carriage to Holbourn made its way up Beechen Cliff and then took a road headed west along a rolling hill to a small estate overlooking Bath. The size of the home reminded Elizabeth of Longbourn, but it was made of the Ashlar stone quarried in the area, and the grounds were more extensive. There was a small cottage off to one side and a large stable partially visible in the back. The crescent design of the streets of Bath had been implemented in the design of the garden walkways.

As the carriage pulled up, Dr. Baldwin emerged from the cottage at the same time the front door of the house opened and a small, middle-aged woman with a round face and friendly smile stepped out.

"James, you didn't tell me we were expecting guests this afternoon!"

"I'm sorry, Mother. I didn't think to mention that the Darcys were coming to visit my laboratory and see my new microscope."

"The laboratory can wait. You must invite them in for tea first."

After introductions were made, Mrs. Baldwin exclaimed to Elizabeth, "It's not every day that a barouche and four arrives at our door. What a delightful surprise. Do come in for tea. If only my forgetful son had told me, I should have had fresh cakes prepared. Young men simply don't understand, or should I say, pay attention to common social conventions. My son is quite brilliant in many ways, but very forgetful in others, I'm afraid."

They were seated in a well-appointed parlour and Mrs. Baldwin took a special interest in Georgianna and Kitty with questions about their stay in Bath and what entertainments they had enjoyed. When she learned about their visits to the Upper Assembly, she asked if they knew her older son as well. When they answered affirmatively, she stated, "I'm not surprised that you've met Tom for he loves to go out in society and he especially loves to dance." To this the young ladies agreed that he was, in fact, an excellent dancer.

While enjoying tea and biscuits they were then introduced to Mr. Thomas Baldwin. He was tall like his younger son, James, with the same dark eyes, strong jaw, and distracted look, but he greeted them cordially, asked their opinion of Bath architecture, inquired where they were staying, and if they had been to Pultney Street and Sydney Gardens. He nodded approval at their complimentary replies and then excused himself.

On their walk to the cottage, Dr. Baldwin remarked that his mother and brother resembled each other in looks and attitude as they were the genial, outgoing members of the family, while he and his father were more introverted and bookish by nature. Kitty inquired if his brother was there but, to her disappointment, was informed that he was out riding.

"I fear I shall be scolded twice over for failing to inform both my mother and my brother of your planned visit. I'm afraid I was only thinking of showing you my new microscope."

The cottage was adjacent to the house and made of the same Ashlar stone. It was well-lit with windows on all sides and inside there were shelves which held an assortment of books, papers, manuscripts, glass jars, and a countertop with vials, glass tubes and small, flat, glass rectangles. At the back of the room was a table on which stood a large black instrument, the recently arrived new microscope, next to another smaller one.

"Anton van Leeuwenhoek built the first microscope in 1674," Dr. Baldwin informed them. "It had only one lens, but he was able to examine blood, yeast, insects, and even pond water. He was a self-taught Dutch scientist and experimented in crafting lenses that allowed him to examine cellular and multicellular organisms such as those seen in pond water. I follow his practices to examine water from the hot springs so I can extract and understand the different mineral components, in hopes of determining which are most beneficial to my patients. Would you like to look through the lens?"

Georgianna was the first to take a turn and examine specimens on the small rectangular glass trays. She gasped with amazement at the beauty of the wing of a fly. After a moment, she lifted her head, looked directly at Dr. Baldwin and said, "It's quite fascinating isn't it? To think a pesky little insect that we swat away when they annoy us, could be so beautiful under magnification? The wings are like gossamer, covered with tiny rainbows of colour when seen so close up." Dr. Baldwin beamed and nodded back.

Darcy was next to examine and asked many questions as he studied the glass slides. He was followed by Elizabeth, who found it most remarkable and then by Kitty. All of them marvelled at what they saw, and it added greatly to the respect and admiration they felt for Dr. Baldwin. He in turn was flushed with pride in response to their approbation. Darcy inquired why Dr. Baldwin didn't have the laboratory at his office in Bath to which the doctor replied that his home and office weren't spacious enough to accommodate the many accoutrements to his scientific study, so he split his time between his practice in town and his research at Holbourn.

On their way back to Bath, Darcy commented it was unfortunate that Dr. Baldwin had to traverse the distance between his home and the laboratory as it would be so much more convenient to live in a space that would accommodate both. Georgianna concurred, saying he could accomplish so much more with an expansion of space for his research. Kitty's only regret was that they didn't get to see Tom Baldwin or any of the horses or dogs of which he was so proud. That evening, as Elizabeth walked down the hallway, she overheard Georgianna and Kitty talking.

"Oh, Kitty, what did you think of the laboratory? I was entranced by the experience and I must declare that Dr.

Baldwin is the most amiable man of any of my acquaintance. He is so interesting and intelligent that I could listen to him all day. I don't feel the least bit shy in his company and I can easily converse with him. He's so kind and caring with everyone that I can't help but esteem him more than any other man I know. Somehow, I feel safe with him. I felt that way once before with someone I should have been able to trust, until I learned that I was woefully mistaken about his character."

"We were all mistaken about Mr. Wickham and yet now my sister, Lydia, is married to him. How capricious life can be. Anyway, I believe you are far more entranced with Dr. Baldwin than you are his laboratory," giggled Kitty. "For my sake, that is just as well, since it leaves you no time for Mr. Willoughby, who may not be as intelligent, but is certainly more handsome and oh so charming. I think him the most charming man in all the world. I would be ever so happy if he paid his addresses to me, although I think your brother had other ideas when he first introduced him to us. I am quite certain he harboured hopes that Mr. Willoughby would be the one to capture your affections, Georgie. Lah-de-dah, I do believe I should even learn to play the instrument as you do just to hear him sing."

"That would not do, Kitty, for then you wouldn't be able look at him while he sang," Georgianna laughed.

"I could look at him all-the-day long if only I had the opportunity; he seems so sincere, poor man, and so alone . Do you know that the last time he visited Bath he met a young lady with whom he formed an attachment? He spoke with great openness about his broken heart when her guardian intervened and cut off all contact between them, for at the time he had not come into his inheritance. Oh, Georgie, he even said I reminded him of her! That I resembled her in height and colouring and then he said she was quite lovely. Can you imagine? Quite lovely! My heart was in my throat as he spoke, and he looked so sad and wistful that I wanted to reach out to comfort him. It was only after he'd given up hope of seeing the young lady again that he married an heiress who later died in childbirth. It's all so terribly tragic, isn't it? It would be my fondest wish to bring joy back into his life if he would only let me. And he's already wealthy so my small dowry need not be an impediment. Of course, your brother may not take kindly to such a liaison, but then again, nor would he force you to marry someone for whom you had no genuine feelings as you do for Dr. Baldwin."

"Be careful with your heart, Kitty. Do not give it so freely that you endanger your good name and that of your family."

Elizabeth could not help but feel deep concern over the revelations of their conversation. She was hardly surprised to hear Georgianna express her feelings for Dr. Baldwin but was distressed to hear how smitten Kitty was with Mr. Willoughby. Why would a man of conscience dally with a young woman like Kitty so soon after losing his wife during childbirth? She was further vexed that he would share such an intimate story of an attachment to another young lady when last he visited Bath, especially by comparing the two young women. Could he possibly have any serious intentions towards Kitty? It seemed unlikely for while she was pretty of face and figure, she lacked wealth and social standing to make her attractive to a man of consequence, especially in comparison to Georgianna. Would he choose a flirtation with the one if he couldn't win the other? Elizabeth would have to hold these thoughts close to her heart considering the angst it would cause her husband, for if he found out that the very gentleman whom he hoped to attach to his sister could be so inconstant, he would be much aggrieved. She would also have to keep a much closer eye on her younger sister and be watchful of the attentions of Mr. Willoughby for she could no longer consider him a trustworthy escort for those young ladies as she had before.

Chapter 15

A few days after the excursion to Holbourn, they visited
the Upper Rooms for another evening of music and
dancing. The season was in full swing and the room was
crowded as they squeezed their way through the entry and
began the competition to carve out places to sit and view the
floor, that still allowed for carrying on an audible
conversation. Mr. Willoughby had joined them and despite the
crowds, he managed to arrange for a location to suit their
needs. When the next dance commenced, he invited
Georgianna to be his partner and led her to the floor. Before
long, Dr. Baldwin and his brother arrived, and Thomas
escorted Kitty to the floor.

"I was most sorry to miss your visit, when I rode out to see
the colt that John Thorpe was offering," he stated. "As I recall
it was you who made the recommendation that I should
consider it when I first introduced you to Mr. Thorpe. If my
brother had informed me, you would be visiting, I would have

made a point of being there. James can be forgetful sometimes and overlook social courtesies, but my mother was delighted to meet you although disappointed that she was not better prepared for she dearly loves to entertain."

"Did you decide to purchase the colt? I believe there was a terrier puppy offered to sweeten the deal."

"I did indeed and must congratulate myself as it was an excellent bargain on both counts. I hope to introduce you to them very soon, for you must come visit again," he replied.

"Your mother was a most amiable hostess, and I must admit that I had rather hoped to have seen your dogs and horses more than to look through a microscope, although I found it more interesting than I would have imagined. Georgie was quite taken with it, but I believe I prefer the company of puppies over pond water," replied Kitty with a bright smile.

As Darcy and Elizabeth looked on, they discovered the arrival of Captain Wentworth and Admiral Croft with their wives and immediately invited them to join their party. The admiral commented that he wasn't a dancer but had come along at the insistence of the ladies. It was their first visit to the Upper Assembly since their arrival.

"The music is so loud one can hardly hear oneself think and my leg is too gouty to dance," he declared. "Still, I'm grateful for a comfortable viewing spot and good company for conversation, such as can be achieved in such a crowded hall. The ladies must have their pleasures and the opportunity to display their fashionable frocks, and it is our duty to accompany them, isn't that right, Frederick?"

"Quite right," answered Captain Wentworth, "and I believe I may do more service to my wife's lovely new gown if I escort her to the floor so all may see her, for she is looking particularly beautiful this evening," and he smiled proudly as he escorted Anne to the floor.

When the set was over, Willoughby brought Georgianna back to their party and he was introduced to the Crofts. The Wentworths rejoined them as well and when the next dance commenced, Willoughby invited Kitty to be his partner to her great delight. Dr. Baldwin had already escorted Georgianna to the floor where they engaged in as much conversation as the dance and music allowed. Finally, the call to tea came and they pressed their way through the crowd to a table that had been arranged in advance by Willoughby.

"What a good fellow," declared Admiral Croft. "I respect a man who plans in advance for the comfort of the ladies and shall take the opportunity to sit with them."

Willoughby bowed graciously at the compliment and then began a conversation with Mrs. Croft, for he was eager to hear more about her travels which Elizabeth had revealed to him earlier. The three of them, along with Mrs. Wentworth, engaged in a lively conversation while Kitty and Georgianna stood talking to Dr. Baldwin, his brother, and some of their other acquaintances.

"Women may be quite as comfortable on board a man-of-war as they are in the finest of homes in England," declared Mrs. Croft. "I have travelled with my husband on five ships altogether and I can assure you that the accommodations are quite the equal of any I have enjoyed on land." The conversation then turned to their various destinations and Willoughby inquired as to which was her favourite.

"Gibraltar is a beautiful place and the weather is wonderfully temperate. The prospect of the Mediterranean from a hilltop is quite as breathtaking a view as you will ever find; you can see all the way to North Africa. I was blessed that, unlike my brother, who is opposed to having women on board, my dear husband welcomed my companionship and allowed me my share of the adventure."

When it was announced that the music would begin again, they all adjourned to the main hall as partners made their way to the floor. Elizabeth was standing beside Anne Wentworth and Mrs. Croft facing Mr. Willoughby, who was still taking a curious and amiable interest in the tales of adventure shared by the admiral's wife. The only thing that could have added greater felicity to the moment was the sight of Colonel Brandon and his wife. Elizabeth was eager to introduce these new acquaintances to their party and beckoned for them to join her.

As Marianne was in the lead ahead of her husband, she approached the group first, at which point Mr. Willoughby turned around with a genial smile to greet the new arrivals. Marianne's face blanched white with shock and dismay.

"Willoughby! What are you doing here?"

The shock on Willoughby's face was equal to her own and he managed to stammer out the words, "Marianne! Forgive me, I mean Mrs. Brandon. What a surprise to see you and Colonel Brandon. I hope your family is well. Will you please excuse me? I'm engaged for the next dance with Miss Darcy."

He bowed, turned towards Georgianna, who had been chatting with Dr. Baldwin, and escorted her to the floor.

By now, Marianne's face was flushed red and the perturbation of her spirits was evident. Introductions were quickly made to the Wentworths and the Crofts, but after a few moments, Marianne announced the onset of a headache, begged their leave, and her husband escorted her hurriedly from the hall. Elizabeth was astonished at what had transpired and could not contain her curiosity at the strange encounter. She observed that Willoughby looked equally flushed and ill at ease as well. His usual courtly manners and easy smile were no longer in evidence as he danced with Georgianna and to Kitty's great disappointment, when the dance ended, rather than inviting her to the next, he made his excuses for leaving early and departed.

That evening at home, Elizabeth could find no other subject to discuss but the strange encounter between Mr. Willoughby and the Brandons.

"Surely they know each other. That was quite apparent. They were equally shocked by the encounter; he even called her by her first name and he asked about her family."

"I was engaged in conversation with Captain Wentworth and paid almost no attention until they departed so hastily. I didn't observe the encounter until it was over, although I could not help but notice the agitation on Willoughby's part as he made a hurried exit," replied Darcy.

"Oh, this is a very strange business, very disconcerting, and I don't know what to make of it. I don't wish to pry but am sure my curiosity will plague me until I am better able to understand the peculiar encounter, and I do hope Mrs. Brandon will call on me soon to give an explanation. Do you think it advisable to make inquiries of Mr. Willoughby? He was equally distressed and left very abruptly. We've welcomed him so openly but, in retrospect, we know very little of him."

"Let us get some rest, my dear, and discuss the matter tomorrow. It is, indeed, perplexing but we shall have no answers tonight."

Early the following day, Elizabeth received a note from Marianne that she would call later that morning and Elizabeth knew not what to expect, although she was grateful an explanation would soon be forthcoming. At the appointed time, Marianne arrived, and her gaze was downcast as she began to speak.

"I'm sure you could not help but notice the strangeness of my behaviour last evening and my abrupt departure. I feel I have an obligation to explain my actions and entreat you to listen to my story full through. I hope that my request does not importune you for I have much to share and beg your patience to listen.

"I must start a few years ago when my family first moved to a cottage at Barton from our father's estate at Norland Park in Sussex, where my two sisters and I had been raised. Our father passed away and our brother from his first marriage inherited the estate, so we were obliged to move with our mother to a cottage near our cousins. Shortly after arriving there, while out for a walk, I injured my ankle when I stumbled down a hillside and Mr. Willoughby came to my rescue and carried me back to the cottage. That is how our acquaintance began.

"I will confess there was an instantaneous affinity between us and, to be frank, we both erred against the usual rules of decorum between new acquaintances, because we shared so many common interests and opinions. Where I should have been more reserved, I was open and sincere and believed him to be as well. He quickly became a daily visitor and all who saw us together speculated that our attachment would lead to an engagement. For me he unified all my ideals of manly perfection in looks, tastes, manners, opinions and, rather than being ruled by propriety, I gave my heart without reservation, believing that he did the same.

"The day came that he announced his aunt, whom he was visiting and whose estate he was to inherit, had ordered him to London with no prospect of returning any time soon. I was devastated and inconsolable, but, as I looked back on our conversations, I could not fault him, for he had made no promises to me. Even my dear mother thought we were engaged save for making the announcement. Everyone saw me as the injured party, but I had only injured myself by being so open and trusting rather than reserved and sensible of propriety.

"My sister, Elinor, and I were invited to travel with our cousin, Mrs. Jennings, to London as her guests which raised my hopes of seeing him again and rekindling our affection. I sent letters announcing my arrival but he neither replied nor visited. At last, I did encounter him at a party, and much like you saw last evening, he greeted me politely and excused himself to rejoin his group. It was announced a few days later that he was engaged to be married to a wealthy heiress and shortly thereafter, he wrote to apologise for any unintended injury and returned all my letters as well as a lock of my hair.

"While travelling back to Barton, we stayed at an estate named Cleveland near his home, Combe Magna. I became gravely ill after taking an extended walk in the rain in hopes of viewing where he lived, so great was my torment. My sister, Elinor, was caring for me at the time and revealed that he called at Cleveland when he learned I was nearby and ill. He confided to her that his feelings for me had been sincere, although he had no choice but to select a wife whose wealth could support his expensive habits and satisfy his aunt's expectations. Shortly after, they were married. Now you understand the shock of unexpectedly meeting him last evening."

"I am so sorry for your suffering," said Elizabeth. "He is a handsome man with charmingly open manners that easily captivate others, but I'm sure such a betrayal of your trust must have come as a great shock."

"Yes, that is true, but I really must look to myself as the cause of my own suffering. At the time I gave way too eagerly to my heightened sensibilities and ignored all claims of sense and propriety. I came to terms with that lesson upon realising that his expensive habits required financial support and a marriage to me would have inevitably faltered for want of income. It would have led to resentment and discontent in the end, but this is only part of the story."

"Pray, go on."

"Colonel Brandon was witness to the budding relationship and my preferment for Mr. Willoughby, and it was a source of great concern to him for an entirely different reason. I have his permission to share the source of his consternation, which I hope you will undertake to judge separately. It is a story he first shared with my sister, Elinor, while we were still in London.

"My husband grew up with someone he dearly loved who was under the guardianship of his father. They were very close and considered eloping after they learned she was to be married to his older brother, who had little regard and no love for her. They were separated, he was sent away, and she was forced into a loveless marriage. His affection for me was excited by my resemblance to her in looks and manner for we were very much alike: affectionate, lively, unreserved, with open and trusting hearts. While he was away, her inheritance was spent, the marriage failed, and she fled. When he returned some years later, he searched for her everywhere and finally discovered her in a very bad way, dying of consumption, penniless, with a three-year old daughter, Eliza. He took the girl under his care, enrolled her in a school and she often visited his home at Delaford, which he inherited after his brother died.

"At the age of 14 he removed Eliza from the school and put her in the care of a respectable woman charged with overseeing several other young girls of the same age. Not long thereafter, in answer to the young lady's pleading, he made an imprudent decision, and allowed Eliza to travel in the company of her dear friend, and the girl's well-meaning father, who came here to Bath for his health. The two girls were allowed to wander freely, unaccompanied, and with little supervision. Then his ward, Eliza, disappeared entirely and her young friend refused to be forthcoming as to her whereabouts or associations.

"It was fully eight months later before he had word of her and found Eliza seduced and abandoned by the very same Willoughby, who was at that time trifling with my affections in Barton. The scoundrel had left her alone and penniless with no way to reach him after making promises to return for her. As you can imagine, recalling that I once longed to marry a man of such low moral character is an abomination to me now. Had my heart's desire come true, and I later learned of his deceit, I would have been attached to a man whom I could no longer respect.

"I hope that you appreciate my unreserved candour in sharing this information with you. After our recent conversation, when you told me that Mr. Darcy had a new acquaintance whom he considered to be a suitable match for his sister, to see Willoughby escorting Miss Darcy to the dance floor last evening, knowing he was likely that very suitor, compelled me to seek you out at the earliest possible moment."

Elizabeth was aghast with the news and expressed her greatest respect and appreciation for Marianne in taking her into her confidence. Elizabeth commented that she always found it strange that she had never observed any indication or expression of grief by Willoughby at the loss of his deceased wife and child, which was surely yet another indicator of his moral deficits.

"I am so grateful to have made your acquaintance and want to thank you again for your gracious invitation to play your instrument regularly during my stay. It was most kind of you and added greatly to the felicity of my visit to Bath. You once asked me how it is that I learned to play with such passion," said Marianne. "I believe I have learned not to wear my emotions so openly as I once did and to express them through the music instead."

Elizabeth sat in stunned silence after Marianne departed. With great perturbation of mind, she wondered what to do next. Of course, her husband must be told immediately, but what were they to say to Kitty and Georgianna? How were they to detach from Mr. Willoughby who had become so much a part of their daily activities and discourse, for clearly the relationship must come to an end. A partial answer to her questions came quickly for a note from Willoughby was delivered into her hands that same afternoon.

Dear Mr. and Mrs. Darcy,

I regret to inform you that I have been called away on an important business matter that will occupy my time for the immediate future and have no intention of returning to Bath anytime soon. I wish to thank you for so graciously welcoming me into your home and express my great enjoyment in meeting you and your delightful sisters. Please give my regards to Miss Darcy and Miss Bennet and express my regrets for not bidding them farewell in person.

Sincerely,

John Willoughby

Elizabeth was grateful that her husband returned home earlier than their sisters and relayed all that she had learned from Mrs. Brandon, along with showing him the note from Mr. Willoughby. His shock was equal to her own for it rekindled past grievances and injuries suffered at the hands of another scoundrel, whose actions had proved the extent of damage an opportunistic man of little character can do by taking advantage of the trust and innocence of a guileless young girl. Upon reading it, Darcy shook his head with disgust and repulsion.

"I should have listened to you instead of giving way to my pride, Elizabeth. I am mortified to realise that I took so little care when I introduced such a man into our midst with no more thought than for his fine looks, charming manners, and the eligibility of his purse, rather than for the quality of his character. He probably has not visited Bath since he seduced a free-spirited young lady with no discernable supervision or protection, whom he callously turned around and discarded. To think I put our own sisters at risk to such a man. I am heartily ashamed. This is yet more evidence of the error of judgement caused by letting first impressions guide your decisions with no further need for discernment."

"You mustn't disabuse yourself for you meant well and we were all under the sway of his easy charm," replied Elizabeth. "But what do we tell Kitty and Georgianna? Kitty was quite smitten with him and might easily have fallen victim to his influence should he have directed his interest towards her. I will be forever grateful to Mrs. Brandon for her candour and concern in sharing such personal, delicate information, but I wonder if we need to share all we know?"

"I quite agree, the less said the better for now. Let the note speak for itself and say as little as possible. Georgianna has not been importuned, for I have reluctantly observed that her attentions run in another direction entirely. Kitty is young and will soon find another to interest her. We must dismiss Willoughby's departure as though it is of little concern and privately count our blessings that he is no longer available to make mischief with any young ladies of our acquaintance."

When they dined that evening, Darcy announced they had received a note from Mr. Willoughby about his immediate departure. As expected, Kitty was greatly distressed and asked many questions. Where had he gone? Why had he left? Would he return soon? Would they invite him to Pemberley some day? None of the answers satisfied her and there was no attempt to raise her expectations. She and Georgianna retired early, the one to console the other for her dashed hopes and broken dreams. Darcy and Elizabeth, on the other hand, breathed a sigh of relief that Kitty had not suffered any greater injury than an inconsolable heart which would soon mend.

The next day, Georgianna sought to comfort her friend by playing cheerful music but that only increased the discomfort of Kitty who was reminded of Willoughby's singing. Shopping was out of the question and even a visit to the Pump Room held no interest. There was nothing to be done but wait for the mood to pass.

Chapter 16

A week after the departure of Willoughby, the Bath newspaper announced the arrival of the Dowager Viscountess Dalrymple and her daughter, the Honourable Miss Carteret, who would be residing at the Royal Crescent during their stay. A mention was also made that Miss Elizabeth Elliot, daughter of the recently deceased Sir Walter Elliot, Baronet, principle seat of Kellynch Hall, Somerset, had also accompanied them.

Elizabeth had anticipated meeting Miss Elliot ever since she came to know something of the former occupant of Camden Place through her new acquaintances with Lady Russell and Mrs. Smith. She did not expect to find Miss Elliot agreeable by nature or upbringing for it seemed certain she would be not just vain and haughty, but also that she would be aggrieved. She had spent much of her life at the head of the line alongside her father, Sir Walter, indulged, indolent, superior, and now she found her circumstances greatly diminished at the hand of the very man who inherited the family estate, Sir William Elliot, and his conspiring, duplicitous new wife.

Her curiosity was soon to be satisfied for she received an invitation to visit Lady Russell the very day of the newspaper announcement. Having heard that Miss Elliot would be a guest at Lady Russell's when she arrived back from Ireland, Elizabeth fully anticipated that she would be there. She arrived at the appointed hour and found Lady Russell in the parlour along with Anne Wentworth and Elizabeth Elliot. Never had she found two people more dissimilar than these two sisters. She had long presumed that Miss Elliot would be considered the handsomer of the two, but she could not agree to such an attribution, for Anne Wentworth was not only very pretty, but combined that with intelligence, warmth, and good humour.

Miss Elliot, now in her early thirties, was taller than her sister with a porcelain complexion, large eyes, well-proportioned features, and the regal bearing of someone used to the approbation of others. She was elegantly dressed and graceful in her movements, while conveying a sense of superiority in her manner and speech.

"Mrs. Darcy, how have you enjoyed your stay at Camden Place? I do hope it met your expectations of elegance and comfort. My father and I did a good deal of planning and spared no expense in the fitting-up of the place for he insisted on perfection in everything to which he turned his attention."

"We are delighted with the house, Miss Elliot. Your excellent taste is fully on display throughout and adds to the amiability of living there. Thank you for asking."

"Elizabeth, tell us of your stay with our cousins, the viscountess and her daughter. How did you find Ireland?" asked Anne.

"The landed nobility I found acceptable if not superior society, but much of the country is overrun by Papist peasants who are exceedingly indolent, when they're not rioting and fighting. They want restraint upon their passions and do everything excessively whether it's their poetry, their songs, dancing, or drinking. One must avoid them whenever possible. You have never in all your life seen as many people with flaming red hair and freckles. Our father would have been appalled for he hated freckles, and their speech, their Irish brogue as they call it; one can hardly understand a word they say!

"The viscountess is exceedingly dull company on her own but does make an effort to go out into society often and has a large number of acquaintances. The estate is handsome though small, since her son inherited the larger estate, and the grounds are beautifully designed, but lack the refinement one finds in English gardens. Of course, as a guest, I held my tongue on such matters as these. Catherine Carteret is hardly better company than her mother and the plainest young woman I have ever set eyes on. She has little by way of conversation and spends all her time reading or walking in the gardens. She has no particular talents to speak of and shows little evidence of superior taste. My efforts to guide her towards exhibiting a more fashionable appearance were vastly unappreciated and so her attire matches her plainness still.

"If I had not been in mourning for our dear father, I should have gone mad with boredom, but one must demonstrate proper respect for the loss of a loved one and withdraw socially, unless an important invitation comes along. Dublin offers many entertainments but, of course, it cannot compare to London, and Ulster is known for the finest linens in all the world. They do beautiful needlework there and the lace making is quite extraordinary as you can see on my sleeves and collar." All agreed that the lace was exquisite.

"Mrs. Darcy, may I ask how you made the acquaintance of our dear Lady Russell?"

"My husband had business in London, so I travelled here with our two younger sisters, and he joined us shortly thereafter. He thoughtfully arranged for Mr. Shepherd to show us the house when we arrived, and it was Mr. Shepherd who made the introduction to Lady Russell and Dr. Baldwin."

"Dear Dr. Baldwin. He was so kind and attentive to our stricken father, was he not, Anne? He did everything in his power to make our father comfortable and help with his recovery. I am quite fond of him."

Her brow then furrowed, and her lips tightened as she said, "How fortunate for you that Mr. Shepherd was of help upon your arrival and made introductions to such superior society. For myself, I find him to be an odious man at whose hands I have been sorely mistreated by him and his daughter. They are vile, scheming, and duplicitous people.

"You once warned me, Anne, that Mrs. Clay was conspiring to win the heart of our dear father, but that would have been impossible because she was badly freckled with a protruding tooth and our father couldn't abide such flaws.

How could anyone begin to imagine that she was scheming instead to entangle our father's heir? And now she is Lady Elliot! It is abhorrent that she should hold such an esteemed title. How could our cousin have married a woman of such common birth and complete lack of refinement? Of course, he'd married such a woman once before to enrich himself, but Mrs. Clay had nothing to offer except her ability to ingratiate herself.

"I don't wish to importune you, Mrs. Darcy, but by right I should still be in residence at Camden Place, with a proper inheritance to support my living there. I have been meanly used by them all, but please, do not allow this news to detract from your enjoyment of your accommodations."

"Elizabeth, my dear sister, there is nothing to be gained by reviving such thoughts of mistreatment and injustice," Anne soothed. "We must move forward and look to the future."

"Future! What future do I have with no purse to sustain me nor proper dowry to offer a suitor of similar status to myself? But I must apologise, for you are quite right that our guest need not be burdened by my hardships."

"Mrs. Darcy has invited us to their home for a small party. I hope it will not cause you to relive these past grievances should we accept?"

"No indeed! I should quite enjoy a visit and the opportunity to remember happier times when we lived there with father. How very gracious of you to invite us, Mrs. Darcy."

With that, a date was agreed upon and Elizabeth departed. Surely her expectations of Miss Elliot had been well founded but she could not help but feel sorry for her anyway. There was no doubt that a single lady of superior birth burdened by a small dowry and high expectations, would have trouble attracting a suitable husband, for marriage was quite often viewed as a value exchange. Marriage was required of a single woman to avoid being a burden to her family; a dilemma to which Elizabeth Darcy could easily relate.

Chapter 17

Colonel Fitzwilliam arrived like a breath of fresh air, full of good humour, goodwill, and tales of his travels to Bristol. Darcy was especially glad to see his cousin whom he relied on for both thoughtful advice and lively camaraderie. Elizabeth was grateful for her husband's sake as well as her own. They had unfinished business regarding Mr. Willoughby's departure and hoped for his advice. Georgianna was in good spirits, but Kitty was despondent over the sudden removal of the man she so greatly admired.

"Welcome back, cousin," said Darcy. "We've missed your amiable companionship and the humourous anecdotes you always manage to share. What stories have you to tell of your travels?"

"I only went so far as to Bristol as I was very curious to see the new suspension bridge that's been installed over the rivers Avon and Frome. It's quite an ingenious design and a construction marvel. The port is busier than ever with imports coming from Ireland, South Wales, and the Americas, of course. They are daily unloading large quantities of sugar cane, tobacco, cocoa, and, of course, rum. Trade is the engine that drives the kingdom to be sure if Bristol is any example. I considered taking a short excursion to Ireland, for Dublin is a favourite city of mine, but didn't quite find the time. The Irish people are an affable lot and almost anywhere you go, you may rely on the spontaneous outburst of a song or poem from any one at any level of society. It's a jolly experience and I quite enjoy visiting, for they are far less formal and stuffy than we English. A pity we don't treat them better. The north dominates the south, with the Protestant gentry ruling over the peasant Catholics to keep them under the boot.

"At the request of your solicitor, Mr. Varley, I did make the acquaintance of Sir Thomas Bertram and all the final details of the sale have been consummated. I concur with you that he is a very respectable and amiable man, but I'm happy for your sake, to have the business done with at last. He plans to stop over in Bath so I'm sure we'll see him very soon. I believe he wrote to you of his plan?"

"He did indeed, and we expect to entertain him at a small party we have planned with some other new acquaintances. Two of the daughters of the former resident here at Camden Place, a baronet who passed away not long ago, have been invited. One is the wife of a retired naval officer, Captain Wentworth, and the other is yet single. You will be a very welcome addition to our party along with Lady Russell, whom you've met, Dr. Baldwin, and a few others."

"What news of my friend, Colonel Brandon? Are he and

his lovely wife still in town? I do hope they will be in attendance for Mrs. Brandon is a gifted performer and I should be happy to hear her play again."

Here Elizabeth spoke up. "They travelled to Weymouth after the musical soiree at the Sucklings' which you attended and passed back through Bath again for only a few days. We were sorry to see them go for we would have welcomed them wholeheartedly to the party."

"You were expecting another visitor to Bath as I recall, a very eligible young man you met in London, Darcy. Will he be in attendance for I have not met him?"

"Mr. John Willoughby is the man to whom you are referring," replied Darcy with a frown as he and Elizabeth exchanged glances.

"That's the name, Willoughby. You told me he was a very handsome and charming widower, and a highly eligible match for some young lady," he said with a laugh and raised eyebrows. "How have your plans played out on that front? Did your ambitions for Georgianna advance; have any hearts been lost yet?"

"Only one, that of Kitty and, quite fortunately, her heart is only a little broken and quite unharmed," replied Elizabeth.

She went on to tell the full story of the handsome man with the easy charm of whom Kitty had become smitten. All was relayed including the encounter with Colonel Brandon and his wife at the Assembly Hall, and the shocking story Marianne revealed of her past encounters with Mr. Willoughby, and his injurious treatment of the innocent young ward of Colonel Brandon.

"This is very bad business, and it raises some discomfort for I am reminded that young ladies from both of our families were disabused at the hands of another dubious character, Mr. Wickham."

"Those are the very memories that have prevented us from informing Georgianna and Kitty about the true reason for Willoughby's abrupt departure. We are reluctant to revive these unpleasant thoughts and yet feel that perhaps we ought. Georgianna was not taken with him, but Kitty was completely infatuated and has been despondent ever since. How do you advise us? Should we tell all?" asked Elizabeth.

"Kitty is young and will soon have her heart stolen again to be sure. Both these ladies are old enough to be advised of the care they must take with new acquaintances and that not all men who approach have honourable intentions. Better that they be wise and cautious than too readily won over by easy charm and handsome manners. Kitty doesn't seem a likely target but then neither did Lydia. Think if she had followed in her sister's footsteps or been entangled as Georgianna almost was. Perhaps the truth will help mend her broken heart."

"I'm ashamed that it was I who opened the door to the scoundrel," admitted Darcy. "It almost developed into a small conflict with my dear Elizabeth whose observations were far more insightful than my own. One must be careful to never judge a man's character by his looks and the size of his purse. To think I considered him an eligible match for my own sister."

"Georgianna's interests appear to be directed towards

someone else entirely for she and Dr. Baldwin seem quite enamoured with one another," replied Elizabeth.

"Yes, the good doctor. He seems to be a very respectable gentleman of excellent character and is highly regarded in the community from what I've observed. He may be a second son who stands to inherit nothing, but he is educated and self-sufficient and does good in the world. I find more and more that I quite admire him," said Darcy.

"My dear cousin, please do not be so disparaging of second sons, for we face a difficult lot in life," laughed Fitzwilliam. "We can't all inherit grand estates as you did. Some of us must either marry well or take up a trade."

~~*~*

Darcy received a calling card from Sir Thomas Bertram a week later announcing his arrival in Bath. They invited him to dine the next evening not knowing what to expect for Darcy had only met him briefly. He was in his early fifties, still handsome and elegantly dressed, with genteel manners, and was not only well-travelled, but conversant on many topics. The seat of his baronetcy was Mansfield Park and he had two sons and two daughters. His youngest son was married to the niece of his deceased wife's sister and inherited the living at a nearby parsonage. His oldest daughter lived with his deceased wife's other sister, his youngest daughter was happily married, whilst his oldest son remained a bachelor. He informed them his wife had passed away two years earlier, but he was glad to have his family to console him. He planned to stay a week in

Bath and enjoy the local entertainments. He expressed great admiration for Camden Place and inquired about the duration of their stay in town and for descriptions of their estate at Pemberley.

He was quite interested in learning more about the excavation of the Roman ruins for, although he had passed through Bath many times, he'd never taken time to explore them. To everyone's surprise and Georgianna's great delight, she spoke up confidently and offered interesting historical information she learned from Dr. Baldwin. With that, Sir Thomas determined that he would visit the Pump Room and then explore the ruins himself while he was in town. He was amiable company and delighted to find out he would be included as a guest at a dinner party they were planning for the former residents of Camden Place, whose late father was also a baronet.

The date was finalised, and the invitations were delivered the next day. Elizabeth decided to invite Mr. Thomas Baldwin along with his brother, James, thinking it might ease the disappointment of Kitty at the absence of Willoughby, to have another young man in attendance who could be counted on for his amiable disposition and easy conversation. In all the party would consist of Lady Russell, Miss Elliot, Captain and Mrs. Wentworth, Admiral and Mrs. Croft, Sir Thomas Bertram, Colonel Fitzwilliam, and the two Baldwin brothers.

Elizabeth exerted herself to plan a suitably delectable menu and ensure there would be fresh flowers in every room, and fine wines would be served at the selection of her husband. It had been some time since she had entertained, and the house was energised with excitement. Georgianna was eager to shop for a new dress and exhorted Kitty to join her for the expedition. Despite her initial reluctance, Kitty also arranged for a new dress and her spirits began to lift as anticipation built for the gathering. They had met all the guests save one, Miss Elliot, and they were very curious about what to expect.

"Is Miss Elliot as charming as her sister?" asked Georgianna. "Mrs. Wentworth is so amiable that I have to imagine her sister is as well. I'm very interested to hear of her travels to Ireland and how she liked it there for I should like to visit myself someday. I hear she is quite beautiful and elegant; I wonder that she did not marry for she certainly would have been a most eligible young woman as the eldest daughter of a baronet."

"You will soon be able to make the comparison yourself," replied Elizabeth.

"I do so wish Mr. Willoughby was still in town and could have joined us. Think of how pleasant the evening would have been if Georgianna had played while he sang. It would have been most delightful," sighed Kitty. "I wonder if we will ever see him again."

"I think not," answered Elizabeth. "In truth, we don't wish to see him again."

With that she asked the two girls to give her their full attention and relayed to them all that she had learned from Mrs. Brandon. Their shock and dismay were fully visible and their expressions heartfelt. Kitty was most alarmed at the news for she felt the full sting of the past elopement of her younger sister, Lydia, and all the scandal that had befallen her family.

She was, by now, well aware that if Darcy had not interceded to compel Mr. Wickham to agree to the marriage, that Lydia could very easily have suffered the same fate as the ward of Colonel Brandon did at the same age. That Willoughby had deceived her into believing his dalliance with Colonel Brandon's ward had been both innocent and interrupted, importuned her even more. Georgianna was greatly affected as well, for she was old enough to realise how easily she had been taken in by Wickham's attentions to her at a tender age. If her brother hadn't discovered the scheme, she might have ruined her young life with an attachment to a cunning man who only wanted access to her fortune and to cause the greatest of all injuries to her beloved brother. This was a truly cautionary tale for them both.

Kitty was subdued as she considered the subject of her ardour in a new light. Finally, she said, "Thank you, Lizzy, for disclosing the truth about Mr. Willoughby, for I should not wish to waste my days yearning for such an unworthy man. I thought him everything a gentleman should be and could not help my attraction to his fine looks and amiable manner, but I do not think he fancied me, or I might have been at risk of falling victim to his charms and deceptions. Now I can relinquish my attachment and focus my attention on discovering an honourable young gentleman with integrity, who does fancy me."

"Wise words, Kitty," replied her sister.

Chapter 18

The day of the party arrived, and all was made ready. The ladies of the house paid special attention to the arrangement of their hair and the selection of their finest attire. Georgianna expressed happiness that both the Baldwin brothers would be attending so that Kitty would also have someone closer to her age and interests to occupy her. For herself, she was content to spend as much time as possible with Dr. Baldwin, whose company she preferred above all others. With Mr. Willoughby out of the picture, she would not be distracted by his attention and could focus fully on her favourite.

Thomas and James Baldwin arrived first followed by Sir Thomas Bertram and Colonel Fitzwilliam. The Wentworths and Crofts appeared next, with Anne looking particularly lovely on the arm of her husband. It was the first time she had crossed the threshold of Camden Place in some time, and she commented on how little it had changed. Finally, Lady Russell entered the parlour, and, after a pause, Elizabeth Elliot strode into the room with head held high and a composed smile on her handsome face, graciously nodding to all.

Miss Elliot commented on the pianoforte and what a pleasant addition it was to the room. On inquiring who played, Georgianna was identified as the primary performer, although it was mentioned that Mrs. Darcy sometimes used it. After remarking that her sister, Anne, played quite well, it was decided a musical performance would be planned for later in the evening.

Miss Elliot continued examining the two main parlours, commenting on objects that she remembered acquiring with her father. She finally positioned herself next to Sir Thomas and began a conversation.

"I understand, Sir Thomas, that you have also suffered the heartbreak of a loss, your beloved wife of many years. May I express my condolences, for I too understand the pain of losing a loved one. My dear father was the best of men, committed and loyal to his family and, above all else, generous and caring. It was such a painful experience to lose him in the prime of his life."

"I am, indeed, sorry for your loss as well, Miss Elliot. I understand this was your home until your father passed, and this is your first time visiting since that regrettable event. I do hope it isn't the source of rekindled grief for you," replied Sir Thomas.

"On the contrary," she smiled, "I am reminded of the happy times we spent together and his superior taste in creating a domicile that reflected his love of all things beautiful. He was extraordinarily attentive to details, from his person to his surroundings and all who knew him understood this. He was a man of elegance and refinement; an exceedingly handsome man. I am quite reminded of him by you, Sir Thomas. You are of a similar age and carry yourself with the same grace and courtly manner that he did."

Sir Thomas bowed and expressed his thanks for such a compliment. The conversation then turned to his deceased wife. He described her as the prettiest young woman he had ever met, and their courtship had been quick and decisive.

"Once I made up my mind to take her as my wife, nothing would stop me, for her dowry was inconsequential to my decision. She gave me two fine sons and two beautiful daughters. Her death was unexpected; her heart failed her, leaving the family to grieve her loss."

"Grief is a lonely burden to carry, is it not? My admiration for my father, and loyalty to him in his time of need, created a wound of the heart that is difficult to heal. You, of course, understand as few others can." With that, Miss Elliot reached for an elegant linen handkerchief with a delicate lace border and appeared to dab her eyes. Again, Sir Thomas made a slight bow.

"I understand you've just returned from Ireland?"

"Yes, our cousin, the Dowager Viscountess Dalrymple, felt it would be best for me to endure the pain of bereavement in new surroundings and invited me to join her and her daughter, Miss Carteret, at their estate near Dublin."

"I've been to Ireland many times. How did you enjoy your stay?"

"The estate was quite beautiful and offered all the elegant accommodations one would expect in such a such consequential setting. Everyone was very kind, and the viscountess and her daughter did all they could to make my stay comfortable. I will admit though, that standing on English soil is a restorative balm, for I do miss my father's estate, and the proximity to family and friends has raised my spirits. I'm sure you, a baronet, understand the unique importance of ties to hereditary lands."

"Indeed, I do. You are quite right in your assessment. There is no greater feeling of contentment than returning to a family estate and the loved ones who reside there."

Georgianna was engaged conversing quietly with Dr. Baldwin and his brother was having an affable discussion with Kitty, extolling the pleasures of riding.

"Miss Bennet, you must plan to visit Holbourn again soon," said Mr. Baldwin. "My mother insists upon it for she would like all your family to dine with us some afternoon, and I should like to show you around the estate so you can see my menagerie. I acquired that colt that I went to see on the day of your last visit and my terrier just delivered puppies. She's even taken the pup that I got from Mr. Thorpe under her care as well. I'm sure you will be greatly entertained, and my mother would be very pleased to meet you again. James will be delighted as well, for he is always pleased to spend time with Miss Darcy. Please say that you'll come, and we'll plan the scheme between our families."

Kitty gave a bright smile and responded that she was eager to visit again, especially with the prospect of seeing the puppies. She was quite sure that the entire family would agree to such a scheme, and they joined Georgianna and James, who expressed great approbation for a return visit as well.

Lively conversation continued until the call to dine was announced. Sir Thomas escorted Miss Elliot and made sure to sit beside her. Colonel Fitzwilliam followed with Lady Russell and finally all were seated for the meal. The discussion turned to Ireland and both Colonel Fitzwilliam and Sir Thomas expressed their fondness for the country and its many delights. Miss Elliot nodded in affirmation and commented on its beauty, and the kindness with which she was treated while there. After they dined, the ladies made their way back to the drawing room for tea, while the men enjoyed their after-dinner port. When the men rejoined the ladies, Georgianna was pressed upon to perform, to the delight of all, but especially Dr. Baldwin. Anne Wentworth proved herself to be a very fine performer as well. Elizabeth was finally coerced into a duet with Georgianna for she felt the exhaustion of a hostess from all the preparations she had overseen.

The party was a great success, the guests were generous in their praise, wishes for future such encounters were expressed, and special thanks were made to the Darcys for organising the delightful event. Sir Thomas was encouraged to call at Lady Russell's and gladly accepted the invitation much to the great satisfaction of Miss Elliot.

Chapter 19

An invitation arrived from the Baldwins to join them once again at Holbourn and a week later they found themselves once again climbing the hill to the Baldwin estate. Mrs. Baldwin expressed her great delight at seeing them again and relief that this time she was able to properly prepare for her guests. She was quite charming and affable, paying much attention to Georgianna and Kitty, inquiring about their interests and enjoyments. She expressed admiration to Georgianna for her talents at the pianoforte' which James had praised and approved her interest and enthusiasm for learning more about the sciences. Ordinarily shy, Miss Darcy was open with her opinions and interests and spoke confidently. After the meal was served, the young people excused themselves to go explore the grounds, while the Darcys stayed behind to continue the conversation with the Baldwins about the merits of Bath and their enjoyment of the surrounding area.

Elizabeth could not help but observe that while their temperaments were very different, Mr. and Mrs. Baldwin presented a very convivial pairing of opposites. Sometimes those differences in disposition can result in positive outcomes such as her relationship with Darcy, but other times it could result in a long-term mismatch such as her own father and mother. In this instance, Mrs. Baldwin's affable, outgoing nature counterbalanced Mr. Baldwin's reserved and introverted nature resulting in a balance that suited them both. He, like his son, became more animated when the subject of discussion was of particular interest, especially as it pertained to architecture, geology, and family history. While he admired his older son's focus on riding, dog breeding, and other amusements, he had a greater affinity for the interests of his younger son and clearly took pride in him. His earnestness when discussing the contributions his son was making to scientific pursuits and the betterment of health outcomes was clearly heartfelt.

"My James has done more to help the citizens of Bath with his scientific studies and medical practice than anyone I know. His efforts have drawn other practitioners to our city who wish to study and learn from him, and he has become quite renowned even as far away as London."

"Indeed, my wife has definitely benefited under his care, and she goes regularly for treatments, don't you, Elizabeth?"

"I am most grateful for his care and kind attention to me since our arrival," replied Elizabeth, "and his enthusiasm for his studies seems to be contagious; it has opened new areas of interest to Miss Darcy. She even purchased a book on herbal remedies to study about plants. She has grown much more confident in sharing information and anecdotes based on the knowledge he has imparted to her, and it has been a revelation to see."

As Elizabeth stood up so they could go examine the grounds, she suddenly felt faint and had to sit down again. Mrs. Baldwin brought some water to refresh her and she soon recovered. They made their way to the stable where they found Kitty and Tom Baldwin examining the new terrier puppy from Mr. Thorpe. Pleased to see them and eager to impress, Tom opened a stable door, fitted a bridle on a yearling colt, and walked him out of the stall. The animal was too young to be ridden yet, but Tom spoke proudly of the size, markings, gait and movement, bloodlines and heritage. Like his mother, he had a ready smile and warm regard for his guests. He grabbed a handful of nearby hay, handed it to Kitty, so that she could feed the animal, and all could stroke the soft muzzle and forelock.

"I missed your first visit here when I rode out to meet John Thorpe, who was eager to sell this fellow. He won the beast in a card game but couldn't afford the keep so he pressed me to buy it. And, since Miss Bennet recommended that the purchase would 'add to my felicity'," he said with a smile, "I could hardly refuse. Between the horse and the terrier pup I struck a grand bargain thanks to her. He's built for running, this one is and he's a beauty too with the white blaze and stockings against the sorrel. I'm sure he'll be 17 hands high at least by the time he reaches full size. Do you ride, Miss Bennet?"

"I've not had much opportunity to ride but greatly enjoyed the experience when I did have the chance."

"The next time you visit, I'll pull out our old mare, Molly, and saddle her up for you. She's quite gentle for an inexperienced rider," replied Tom with a grin.

"Oh yes! That would be wonderful," Kitty beamed with an elated smile.

Darcy and Tom began a conversation about the bloodlines of horses, their conformation and fitness for hunting or racing. Elizabeth inquired after the whereabouts of Georgianna and Dr. Baldwin from Kitty, who replied that they had headed to the laboratory to look at more specimens. Elizabeth once again noticed a dizziness standing in the sun and suggested to Darcy that they make their way towards the laboratory as well.

When Darcy and Elizabeth arrived at the cottage, they could see the young couple through the window standing close together with him looking down as he spoke until she looked up and they held gazes. The knock at the door startled them and Dr. Baldwin came to open it, inviting them in. Elizabeth was glad to be indoors again and took a seat on a stool as she recovered from the heat of the day. When Dr. Baldwin commented that she looked peaked, he was informed that she had experienced another dizzy spell earlier that day.

"Are you otherwise quite well?" he asked. Her affirmative reply brought a small smile to his face and he suggested that it may be time for her to return home and take a rest. With that they sent for Kitty, paid their respects to Mr. and Mrs. Baldwin with profuse thanks for the amiable afternoon and climbed into the carriage.

"Oh, Georgie, we must visit again soon, for Mr. Baldwin has promised to teach me to ride! Wasn't it a perfectly brilliant afternoon? I can't think when I've had so much fun that didn't include dancing. Mr. and Mrs. Baldwin are quite charming are they not?"

Georgianna nodded agreement but her attention was preoccupied with other thoughts, and she stared out of the window of the carriage with a faraway expression, caught in her own private reverie.

When they arrived home, Elizabeth took a short rest to recover her energy and when she arose was suddenly overcome with a momentary spell of nausea, but this too, like the dizziness, soon passed. That evening when they retired the conversation turned to Georgianna and the scene through the window they had witnessed.

"I thought the visit to the Baldwin estate went well; they seem a genteel and amiable family," remarked Elizabeth. "Mrs. Baldwin is very cordial, Mr. Baldwin has a great many interests, and the family history in Bath is very notable on both sides. Our sisters had a delightful time. Did you enjoy yourself?"

"Yes, they are very agreeable society, genuine and unpretentious and I was impressed with the high regard Mr. Baldwin holds for both of his sons, especially James. He is clearly very proud of the accomplishments his youngest son has achieved. I enjoyed exploring the grounds and the animals Tom Baldwin raises. He has a good eye for horseflesh and an innate way with animals, whereas his brother's interests are far more cerebral in general, and very much focused in one direction particularly."

"I do believe a strong attachment has formed between Georgianna and Dr. Baldwin," said Elizabeth.

"Indeed, I cannot deny it and despite my original misgivings, more than anything, I want Georgianna to be happy, and I will not stand in the way of true love. I learned that lesson long ago. If he is her heart's desire, so be it, but I believe other attachments may be forming as well," replied Darcy. "It seems to me that both of our sisters have made conquests. That the Baldwin brothers are deserving young gentlemen from a worthy and respectable family, alleviates any concerns we might have regarding their character and intentions. We shall have to wait and see, but I do believe your hopes for them both may be answered, and they will surely marry for love."

"I believe Mrs. Baldwin recognises it as well. I had the distinct impression that if she were at liberty to do the matchmaking, she has found two very eligible young ladies for both of her sons."

"I think it's safe to say that Willoughby has been forever vanquished from Kitty's thoughts. For that I am grateful as I still can't forgive myself for inviting him into our midst without knowing more about his character and intentions," replied Darcy.

"Do not distress yourself, my love, for it is all in the past and no harm was done. I believe I shall write to Mrs. Brandon and thank her again for revealing her own painful past that very possibly saved us from equal pain."

Chapter 20

Who can explain the laws of attraction that beset a person for whom one source of love and comfort is lost, and yet another arrives to replace it? Such was the case for Sir Thomas Bertram, whose plan for a week-long stay in Bath was extended and then extended again. Word from Lady Russell was that he'd become a daily visitor, much enamoured with Miss Elizabeth Elliot, under the guise of comforting one another's loss, and leading to the first extension of his stopover in Bath. A few tearful looks and the ever-present linen handkerchief to dry her eyes, left Sir Thomas little choice but to stay on.

The second came by way of an invitation to a reception at the Royal Crescent from the Dowager Viscountess Dalrymple. All the guests that attended the party at Camden Place, hosted by the Darcys, were invited at the behest of Miss Elliot, so Sir Thomas had no choice but to prolong his stay yet again. Who, after all, could refuse an invitation from the Dowager

Viscountess Dalrymple and her daughter, the Honourable Miss Carteret for an event at the Royal Crescent? Even Colonel Fitzwilliam decided to stay on.

Such an invitation was cause for another shopping tour to find fashionable new garments elegant enough for the event, an effort which Georgianna and Kitty eagerly pursued. Even Elizabeth had cause to consider a new gown as she found her favourite dress no longer draped as gracefully as it once did and lacked the sophistication that she desired for such an occasion. She still suffered the small bouts of nausea in the morning that quickly subsided and were hardly noticed.

The Baldwin brothers had become regular visitors to Camden Place and were even able to secure permission to bring a chaise to drive Georgianna and Kitty up to the estate so that Kitty could have her chance at riding the mare. The oversight by the gentlemen's parents meant the excursion would be properly chaperoned, which put Elizabeth and Darcy at ease. On one of the shopping expeditions, Kitty even arranged to purchase a proper riding habit for the occasion.

With Miss Elliot staying as a guest at Lady Russell's, Elizabeth didn't visit quite so frequently at Laura Place, but she did manage to spend time with Mrs. Wentworth and Lady Russell over tea at the Pump Room and they all made their way to visit Mrs. Smith who was not able to get around so freely as the other ladies. Such amiable companionship was highly valued by Elizabeth whose closest friend, her sister Jane, she had not seen in several months, although they wrote to each other frequently.

She corresponded with her father as well, who was eager

for news of life in Bath and the activities of his only unmarried daughter, Kitty, whom he hoped was conducting herself respectably and prudently. Mrs. Bennet was still besieged with her nervous condition and other maladies, and complained about not seeing her daughters, but she was less inclined to write letters than her husband, so he was tasked with conveying her sentiments. His letters were filled with concern about the well-being of Elizabeth, and he wrote that his only regret about encouraging her to travel to Bath, was the distance from Longbourn, and his inability to see her as frequently as he did when she resided at Pemberley. Elizabeth assured him that Kitty had behaved with all the decorum he might hope and the bond between her and Georgianna had grown even more close during their travels together. She did not make mention of the growing attachment between them and the Baldwin brothers, not wishing to share anything more than news of their social engagements. She did inform him of the hot spring treatments she had undergone with the guidance of Dr. Baldwin and the kind services he had rendered.

In contemplating all that had taken place since they departed from Pemberley, Elizabeth realised that despite her initial reluctance, that she had greatly benefited from the arrangement. Her circle of acquaintances had grown, and she highly valued the new friendships that had developed, the intimacies that had been shared, and the insights she had gained. The superior society, the entertainments, the walks in the delightful gardens, the soothing relaxation in the baths, all had lifted her spirits and all but banished painful memories.

Her sister and Georgianna had thrived in the setting and at

least one of them seemed destined for a new life that would leave her as a permanent resident of Bath. Georgianna had been a revelation as she overcame her introverted nature and gained confidence in herself and her emerging interests. Who could object to dear Dr. Baldwin as a loving and devoted companion? Even her husband could find no objection, for although he was a second son, Georgianna's dowry would be safe in his hands and provide a comfortable foundation for a life together. That they would become engaged seemed certain. Kitty had also matured and the budding relationship with Tom Baldwin seemed destined to develop into a more permanent attachment. Kitty's dowry wasn't large, but Elizabeth was certain it would not be an impediment to the acceptance of his family, and the future happiness of both their sons. If all of these musings came to be, their trip to Bath could be considered a triumph.

She was delighted that Colonel Fitzwilliam had stayed on as well, for he was such agreeable company; good humoured, well-travelled, well-read, socially adept and an engaging conversationalist. His manners were very much admired and, while not handsome, his society was sought after wherever he went. As the younger son of an earl, he enjoyed the advantages of wealth but was not so independent as to the selection of a wife, for he was expected to marry a woman of fortune. That he was discerning of character and principles had prevented him from forming an alliance based only on the size of a woman's dowry. Elizabeth valued his companionship as much as did her husband for she was able to take him into her confidence and share news she heard from her circle of friends.

The day of the reception arrived, and the young ladies took special care dressing and arranging their hair in anticipation of the approbation that would surely be directed their way. In the superior society that would gather that evening at the Royal Crescent, they were determined to stand out and hoped above all that the private event would include dancing so they would be fully exhibited. Although this was not a formal ball, they were certain that where music was played, dancing would follow.

The Royal Crescent was a splendid building with a grand interior luxuriously outfitted with beautifully appointed rooms and costly furnishings covered in expensive fabrics. A reception line had formed for the guests to greet the dowager viscountess and her daughter on their way to enjoying the delights of mutual approbation from other fashionably attired people, whose manners, speech, and social standing allowed them access to such exclusive company. The grandeur of the building was handsomely matched by the grandeur of the guests who gathered for the occasion.

The Darcys joined the reception line in the company of their younger sisters, Colonel Fitzwilliam, and Sir Thomas Bertram. Dr. Baldwin and his brother arrived a few minutes later and joined them as they waited to be introduced. When they came closer to the head of the line, they discovered that Miss Elizabeth Elliot had stationed herself next to Miss Carteret. She undertook responsibility for introducing her many acquaintances to her cousins and was delighted with her elevated status in that role.

As they waited, Elizabeth shared with Colonel Fitzwilliam

the story of her first encounter with Miss Elliot upon her return from Ireland and made mention of her comments that Miss Carteret was the plainest young woman she had ever set eyes on, with little taste and less conversation, who did nothing but read and walk in the gardens.

"Harsh judgement, indeed, from one cousin regarding another, especially that of a guest towards her host," was his reply. "I shall give you my opinion on whether she is plain or not after we are introduced," he said with a smile.

Miss Elliot was gratified to be the source of introductions to the Darcys and, most especially, to Sir Thomas Bertram. "Allow me to introduce Mr. Fitzwilliam Darcy and Mrs. Elizabeth Darcy of Pemberley; Sir Thomas Bertram, baronet of Mansfield Park; Colonel Edward Fitzwilliam, son of the Earl of Wessex; Miss Georgianna Darcy of Pemberley; Miss Katherine Bennet of Longbourn; Dr. James Baldwin of Bath, who so lovingly cared for my dear departed father, and his brother, Mr. Thomas Baldwin."

She was polite to the rest of their party but singled out the baronet for particular attention, explaining that he was a widower and expressing her sympathies, since they had both lost loved ones so recently.

After moving through the reception line, they spied the Wentworths and Crofts with Lady Russell and immediately joined them. When all of the guests had been greeted, the viscountess circulated around the room nodding acknowledgements and finally retired to a chair so she could sit and observe the festivities she had arranged. She was joined by her daughter who exhibited signs of complete and utter boredom, while Miss Elliot directed her attentions almost exclusively to Sir Thomas.

To the delight of many, the musicians eventually transitioned from quiet background music to that which invited dancing and couples began to gather in the open space of the hall. In no time Georgianna and James along with Kitty and Tom had joined the couples to form a dance line. Elizabeth was chatting with Colonel Fitzwilliam, and they were standing near Sir Thomas and Miss Elliot when she overheard this conversation.

"I believe it is only for the young and young at heart to take to the dance floor on such occasions. Those of us who mourn must take comfort in merely watching the festivities, for the perturbation of our spirits is not easily lifted by the sounds of music and the appeal of dancing," lamented Miss Elliot.

"Come now, Miss Elliot, you are far too young and beautiful to retire so soon from the pleasures of dancing. Won't you join me as my partner? I believe I still remember the steps although it has been some time, for my wife was not fond of dancing in her later years, and I have not had much practice recently. I appeal to you to join me, and we shall both leave our perturbation of spirits behind us for a short time."

Elizabeth watched them join the other dancers and could not resist looking over at Anne Wentworth and Lady Russell to see their reaction, which was to raise their eyebrows and nod their heads at one another as though this came as no surprise. She turned to Colonel Fitzwilliam commenting that it appeared Miss Elliot had made a conquest of Sir Thomas and mentioning that he had extended his stay in Bath twice already.

"Well, I cannot blame him for she is a very pretty woman, although I would much prefer a plain woman with a kind heart and a fine mind than a pretty one with superior airs."

"According to Miss Elliot, the plainest woman of her acquaintance sits right over there. How do you measure her?"

He glanced over at Miss Carteret, grinned at Elizabeth and said, "Even the wall flowers deserve to dance." With that, he strode over to Miss Carteret with an amiable smile on his face, bowed to her and invited her to join him.

Miss Carteret seemed almost startled by his offer as her composure throughout the event had been one of aloofness and indifference, but she looked up at him, then away, and finally with a nod she stood up to take his arm and be escorted to the floor, while her mother looked on with surprise. As they passed, Elizabeth heard him say, "Miss Carteret, I understand you live in Ireland. I've enjoyed many visits to your country and have very fond memories of my time there."

"I'm glad to hear you say it," she replied, "because not everyone here has such warm feelings towards Ireland. I believe my cousin was quite bored during her stay and found little to amuse her."

"I haven't heard her say anything to indicate such displeasure, but I am told on some authority that you are very fond of reading and taking walks in the garden."

"Is this praise or censure? For if it was my cousin who said this, it was surely meant as censure."

Upon hearing this, Fitzwilliam let out a laugh. "I would

never censure a well-read woman, let alone one who enjoys the merits of walking in a fine garden and enjoying the beauty that nature serves up so abundantly."

"I'm afraid my cousin doesn't share your views. She is content to combine an uninformed mind with the conceits of superior taste and self-approbation as her view of the world."

"I've only just met her, but if that is her view, I believe she may conceal it well from new acquaintances. She spoke warmly of her visit and your kindnesses to her."

"I have no tolerance for deceit, but some women are taught subterfuge and to hide their feelings to please others and achieve what they want. I cannot blame her though, for she learned her attitudes and behaviour from her father."

"Harsh criticism, coming from a cousin."

"A distant cousin. The connection with Sir Walter was only recently revived but my mother took pity on Miss Elliot after his death and invited her to stay with us. She was left in difficult financial circumstances as an unmarried woman with expensive tastes and high expectations."

"I take it that you get little enjoyment from these entertainments?"

"These are tiresome affairs that I do my best to tolerate; one can hardly expect to have an intelligent conversation at such an event. I am happily surprised to have such a discourse with you, Colonel Fitzwilliam, for it is most unexpected and I hope you take no offence at my candour."

"How could I take offence at the honesty and forthright comments of an intelligent woman? I find it quite refreshing."

To this final remark, Miss Carteret gave a slight nod and

smile. When the music concluded, he escorted her back to her seat near her mother. No one else, save Sir Thomas, was bold enough to invite Miss Carteret to the floor, for he was intent on making the best possible impression on the exalted cousins of Miss Elliot.

Chapter 21

When they broke fast the next morning, all the talk was of the event the night before; the beautiful fashions on display, the delicious foods that were served, the delight at the opportunity to dance, the rather imperious behaviour of the viscountess along with the aloofness of her daughter, and the wonder at what seemed to be a rapidly evolving friendship between Sir Thomas and Miss Elliot.

"Sir William is very much in danger of having his heart stolen, and I think Miss Elliot may soon find herself the wife of a baronet after all. Their preference for one another was clearly on display and if he stays on two weeks more, I wager that a formal engagement will be announced," commented Elizabeth.

"I wonder how his grown children will receive that news?" replied Darcy. "I understood from Mr. Varley when he introduced me to Sir Thomas, that his eldest son is something of a spendthrift and his eldest daughter was caught up in some sort of scandal, a marital impropriety, that led to a divorce. They may not take kindly to him marrying a woman with a limited dowry even if she is the daughter of a baronet. It has all the markings of an ongoing family dispute. And what becomes of her fortunes should Sir Thomas pass away, for he is some years older than her with grown children? Should she have a child by him, what protections would they have at the hands of his heir?"

"I sense that Miss Elliot's unceasing attention to her own self-interest will carry her, and she will make every effort to secure her fortunes before entering into an agreement once she has an offer of marriage. Whether the union sets off jealousies or ill-will remains to be seen, but I think that domestic disagreements may exceed any hopes of harmony within the family. Surely, she won't refrain from expressing her true opinions once married, that her artifice covers today," responded Elizabeth.

"I was so proud of Colonel Fitzwilliam for inviting Miss Carteret to dance," said Georgianna. "It seemed to be the only portion of the event that she enjoyed for they were engaged in conversation throughout the dance, and he almost laughed out loud at one of her comments. I do not think her so plain as everyone says although she does seem rather aloof and not easily pleased."

"Perhaps she is not so plain, and he is not so blind that he cannot see her merits," replied Elizabeth. "Not all women thrive on pursuit of the latest fashionable attire, new social engagements, and displays of social consequence. She may have an intellect that requires more meaningful occupations than society allows her and take less enjoyment in the conventional pursuits attributed to females. Perhaps women have the capacity for more consequential endeavours than those to which they are confined by the traditional expectations of society, and I wonder if that is why she remains single. As a woman of fortune, she has no incentive to marry unless she finds a match that allows her to pursue her interests and inclinations."

"If amiable companionship, a quick wit, and a curious mind hold any attraction, then Edward would be a well-suited match for Miss Carteret, so long as she is not ill humoured and contrary," said Darcy, to which everyone agreed.

"A fine mind, an open heart, and a kind disposition are all that one could hope for in a marriage," commented Georgianna.

"I quite agree, except that I would add to the list a love of dancing and enough fortune for a comfortable living," replied Kitty with a smile. "Lizzy, last evening Georgie and I were invited to the Baldwins' again this afternoon as I've been promised another riding lesson and Tom, Mr. Baldwin that is, plans to change out the old mare I've been riding for a livelier horse. They're coming by to pick us up in the chaise soon and we'll be home late afternoon. I hope you don't mind the short notice, but we have such fun when we visit, and I so enjoy learning to ride. I'm told I shall be quite the equestrian expert by the end of the season. When I return home, I shall have to ask Papa to buy me a horse and saddle. I'm fortunate that Mrs. Baldwin used to ride in her youth and so a proper side saddle was available for me."

"Very well, Kitty, but do be careful, for you're not an expert yet and the old mare may suit you just as well for a while longer. Don't try to reach beyond your skill level and do please give our regards to Mr. and Mrs. Baldwin when you see them. I certainly hope they are not tiring of your visits."

"Lord, no, Lizzy! They're quite happy to see us and Mrs. Baldwin is always very gracious. She serves us tea and cakes whenever we come."

The afternoon passed quietly until an urgent message from Dr. Baldwin was delivered.

Dear Mrs. Darcy,

Please do not be alarmed but I must inform you that your sister, Miss Bennett, has suffered injuries after falling from a horse while riding with my brother. Let me assure you that I believe she is in no immediate danger. She was briefly knocked unconscious when she fell but recovered within a few minutes, and she suffered an injury to her left ankle; a sprain rather than a fracture. She is alert and resting comfortably in a bedroom under the supervision of my mother. I recommend that she rests here for a few days so I can monitor the contusion to her head and ascertain that there is no lasting damage. Also, her ankle must be kept elevated to contain the swelling and she should not put pressure on it for several days.

I know how concerned you will be upon receiving this message and that you will wish to see her right away. May I suggest that before you leave, you prepare a valise with garments and sundries for both Miss Bennett and Miss Darcy, who has already insisted that she must stay to look after the patient until she is able to travel.

My mother wishes you to know that she welcomes the opportunity to care for your sister and will extend every courtesy to both the young ladies. She is greatly distressed that the injuries occurred while they were visitors under her charge and wishes to apologise for the distress it must inevitably cause you. I have prepared some remedies for pain and swelling that I will be administering to increase Miss Bennett's comfort and ensure her full recovery. I will personally supervise her medical care with the able assistance of my mother and Miss Darcy.

I remain your humble servant,
Dr. Baldwin

Elizabeth quickly informed her husband of the accident, and she made immediate arrangements for them to visit Holbourn to check on the condition of Kitty. There was no question that she must continue under the care of Dr. Baldwin and that Georgianna must stay there with her dear friend until she could travel.

They were relieved to find Kitty alert and responsive holding a terrier pup in her lap. She was a bit embarrassed by the entire incident, blaming her inexperience as a rider as the source of the trouble. Tom Baldwin was mortified to have allowed the accident to happen under his charge but spoke up in her defence.

"Truly, Miss Bennett was managing the horse wonderfully well and it cannot be helped that the animal was spooked when a grouse was suddenly flushed from the bush and the horse reared up. Miss Bennett did all she could to maintain control and held on as it bucked several times until at last, she slipped from the saddle and wrenched her ankle which remained trapped in the stirrup. I was able to catch the bridle and hold the horse so she wasn't dragged along the ground until I could release her foot. I was desperately torn by whether to leave her there unconscious on the ground to run for help but fortunately, within a few minutes, she recovered her senses and insisted she would be alright until I returned. I didn't dare to move her since I wasn't sure what injuries she had sustained, and I was able to quickly find my brother and bring a wagon so we could bring her back to the house. My mother arranged a room, and I carried her upstairs while my brother saw to her injuries. I hope you can forgive me for the anxiety this has caused everyone, and that Miss Bennett will not be so traumatised by the unfortunate experience that she chooses to never ride again. She was doing so well, even my mother commented on her progress."

"I'm sure I will mend in no time and have every intention of riding again, as well as to purchase a pair of riding boots that would more effectively protect my ankles," replied Kitty stoutly. "I do apologise for the inconvenience and stress this has caused and I'm ever so grateful to the Baldwins for the thoughtful care I have received thus far. I hope Miss Darcy and I won't be too much of a burden for the next few days."

"How can you think such a thing, my dear girl? You mustn't concern yourself in the least and should only concentrate on your recovery," said Mrs. Baldwin. "I'm sure we can't think of any more welcomed guests than you and Miss Darcy, but I do wish to offer my abject apologies to Mr. and Mrs. Darcy for the stress and concern this incident has caused them. Please do forgive our dear Tom and I'm sure he is extremely contrite for being the cause of any injury to Miss Bennett."

Riding back to Bath in the carriage, Elizabeth observed to her husband, "I cannot help but be reminded of my first visit to Netherfield when Jane was taken ill after riding on horseback in the rain at the invitation of Mr. Bingley's sisters to join them for lunch. Do you remember?"

"How could I possibly forget your beautiful face, ruddy from the exertion of walking all that distance, with your hair wild under your bonnet and your petticoat dripping with mud? The very picture of pulchritude," he replied.

"Come, come, you did not think me very beautiful back then. You did everything you could to avoid me the entirety of our stay. How quickly you forget," she said with a smile.

"It's true that I behaved contemptibly while you were there. I believe I was trying to suppress my attraction to you by behaving rudely. I was vain enough to be concerned that if I paid you any attention that it might raise your hopes that I was interested in you, so instead I ignored you."

"I rather thought you might be interested in Caroline Bingley until I observed your dismissal of her assiduous attentions. I remember how she hovered over you as you wrote a letter to Georgianna, admiring your penmanship and wishing you to add messages from her to your sister. It was most amusing to see her efforts at flattery being repelled. I could only assume you considered yourself to be above everyone, including the sister of your friend. You were truly an enigma, but at the time I disliked you so much that I didn't want to know you better and only wished to be home as soon as possible."

"I expect the Baldwins will be far more considerate of their guests and the young men will be eager to shower our sisters with attention. I'm sure their experience will be entirely the opposite of what we felt when first thrown together, between my vanity and your disdain and yet, here we are, the picture of amiability, perfectly happy to be together, and very much in love," he said as he tucked her hand under his arm.

Chapter 22

After a week Kitty was quite recovered and she and Georgianna were just returning from a walk accompanied by James and Tom Baldwin. They were seated in the parlour with Elizabeth when Georgianna, who seemed nervous and distracted, whispered something to Dr. Baldwin, and then went to the instrument and began to play. Dr. Baldwin inquired if Mr. Darcy was at home and was directed that he could be found in the study at which point he stood up, excused himself, and made his way there. Looks were exchanged between Kitty and Tom Baldwin while Georgianna continued to play, although her fingers stumbled over the keys and she lacked her usual proficiency. She managed to play three songs and had begun a fourth when her brother and Dr. Baldwin joined them, at which point she stopped playing and looked up expectantly.

To her relief she saw a broad smile on her brother's face matched by a similar smile from Dr. Baldwin. Darcy asked

Elizabeth if there was any champagne in the house for there was news to share that would require it and he also asked that a note be sent to Colonel Fitzwilliam inviting him to join them immediately.

"Dr. Baldwin has done me the honour of asking for Georgianna's hand in marriage," he announced. "I have given my consent already and only await the arrival of my cousin to confirm that he agrees to the plan, since we share equal responsibility for Georgianna's care. I foresee no objection on his part and want to congratulate the young couple and wish them the same marital joy that I share with my darling wife, Elizabeth. I am certain they are well suited to one another and will enjoy a happy life together."

With that, Georgianna ran to her brother and hugged him. "We promise to be deliriously happy together, incandescently happy!" She then went to stand beside Dr. Baldwin as congratulations were shared by all and the champagne and glasses were delivered to the parlour for the celebration. Georgianna was as jubilant as her fiancé was relieved. Kitty and Tom were overjoyed as was Elizabeth. She had observed the growth of a relationship built on mutual respect and admiration and was happy that their path had been more straightforward than the one that brought her and Darcy together.

Colonel Fitzwilliam soon arrived and, after giving his permission and sharing his own approbation for the match, joined them in the celebration. Elizabeth approached and gently said with a smile, "Are you perhaps somewhat relieved to see Georgianna engaged as it will release some of the pressure from your family to pursue a courtship with her?"

"I could not be happier for dear Georgianna, and I think she and Dr. Baldwin will be a splendid match. I never could contemplate the prospect of making a proposal to someone so young and trusting of me, her guardian, and Darcy was in complete agreement with me, although he would have welcomed me as a brother-in-law had I felt a truly romantic attachment to her. It was out of the question from the start. Since Darcy found his own love match with you, dearest Elizabeth, he could only aspire to a similar outcome for his sister. Granted he had reservations about the young gentleman, not to mention a different suitor in mind, but you brought him to his senses by exposing the true character of that scoundrel."

"I must admit that my concerns about the character of that gentleman caused some friction between my husband and me, but all was resolved by the revelations of Mrs. Brandon, and we were relieved when he departed Bath with such haste. The opportunity to meet the Baldwins and visit their estate also helped turn the tide in favour of the courtship. They are a very respectable family with deep roots in the area and they take great pride in their younger son and his accomplishments. One could hardly overlook such merits let alone observe the growing attachment between the young couple and not embrace the match."

"I will venture to guess that not all family members will welcome the outcome however, as I rather expect that Lady Catherine will disparage the match as entirely unsuitable and be very vocal in her displeasure. I can hear her already in my mind and expect to hear more in person the next time I visit. Indeed, I rather dread the prospect because not only will I have to listen to her deprecations that Georgianna's marital choice was countenanced and approved by her nephew and me, but now she and my family will exert even more pressure on me to propose to her daughter, Anne."

"I do pity your position for I am reminded that second sons who lack an inheritance are in much the same position as young women who lack dowries. Marriage is the only choice to secure a future without being dependent on one's family. I felt the terrible pressure of that when Mr. Collins, heir to my father's entailed estate, arrived at Longbourn in search of a wife. He was determined to make what he considered to be a gracious gesture and select from amongst the five daughters, and my unfortunate lot was that he chose me. My mother was overjoyed with the news that one of her daughters would be the future mistress of the family estate and insisted that I accept the offer. She was determined to eventuate the outcome and when I refused, she swore to disown me and never speak to me again. Fortunately, my father was equally determined that I should not accept a supercilious husband as the price for guaranteeing the future of his estate, and said he would never speak to me again if I did accept the proposal. My father won out and much to my mother's dismay, Mr. Collins went down the road and proposed to Charlotte Lucas a few days later. She willingly accepted the offer so that she would no longer be a burden to her family and after visiting her I concluded that her choice of marriage partner entirely suited her, for she seemed happy and contented. That is when I first became acquainted with you."

"How well I remember and must admit to having been

smitten with you at the time. I believe it pushed my cousin into acknowledging to himself feelings which he had attempted to deny and caused him to press his case to win your love, although he handled it rather badly back then from what I understand, and yet it all turned out well. I hope to someday experience equal felicity in marriage as the two of you have found.

"As to the Collins', I agree they do seem well suited, and I've come to value the company of Mrs. Collins when I visit Rosings, for I see them frequently. As for me, I can't imagine being trapped in an environment dominated by an officious, intrusive, and overbearing mother-in-law were I to marry Anne de Bourgh. My father considers my objections are unessential but what is unessential about choosing a wife for whom you feel love and respect and can live in a harmonious environment? Since I will inherit no estate, I would be bound to reside at Rosings under the remorselessly critical eye of Lady Catherine, yet my father has no appreciation of the sacrifice this would require. For him marriage is contractual and so long as I fulfill my husbandly duties on occasion, I can go where I please and do what I please. If my marriage isn't fulfilling, I should simply seek solace elsewhere with whomever I choose. He doesn't understand the concept of marriage as a union between two people who love and respect one another; who long to spend time together and dread the times when they're not; who match intellect and interests with passion for learning and growing; who can laugh together and enjoy each other's humour. I suppose I'm an idealist, but I hope to someday find such a companion."

Elizabeth nodded in agreement and expressed her sincere hope that this fine man of whom she was so fond, would find the same level of happiness in marriage that blessed her own life. The topic then turned to plans for an engagement party and there were discussions of setting a date. It was decided that the ceremony would take place at Pemberley so that family members and friends could participate. Georgianna would have preferred marrying in Bath without delay but accepted the recommendations since she was eager for her betrothed to see her family home. Where they would live in Bath was also a subject of discussion, but all agreed that a move to a home large enough to contain the laboratory was the most sensible choice and they eagerly looked forward to exploring suitable locations.

The engagement was announced in the newspaper and letters were sent to family members announcing the happy news. Elizabeth even wrote to Marianne Brandon to inform her and to thank her once again for enlightening them about the character of Mr. Willoughby and sparing them such a regrettable connection. Acknowledgements poured in from well-wishers including the viscountess and her daughter, the Wentworths and Crofts, Lady Russell and Miss Elliot; even a note of congratulations from the Sucklings. Of course, Sir Thomas was compelled to extend his stay in Bath yet again so that he could attend the engagement party. Colonel Fitzwilliam's presence was also required for such an important event and thus it was that the plans began to take shape.

Elizabeth wanted to personally deliver the news to Mrs. Smith even though she would have surely read it in the newspaper. She had not visited in a few weeks and being very fond of the intimate friend of Anne Wentworth and Lady Russell, she felt a visit was appropriate, since Dr. Baldwin was so essential in caring for Mrs. Smith's health. When she arrived, Mrs. Smith was already jubilant about the news and grateful for the condescension of a personal visit from Elizabeth.

"It is so delightful that two such fine young people should form an attachment to one another in so short a time. When I think of the years spent apart by Anne and Captain Wentworth and how poor Anne had given up hope of ever being united with the man whom she so deeply loved, it is refreshing to see a young couple so ready to move forward in a life together."

"I don't mean to be presumptuous, but may I ask why was there was such a prolonged separation before the Wentworths married?" asked Elizabeth.

"Have I never told you this? I suppose I thought you knew already. Anne met Captain Wentworth when she was but a girl of 19 and he was on leave, having just returned from the action off St. Domingo, and come to stay with his brother for a few months. They fell deeply in love, but Sir Walter refused to grant permission for the match as he thought it a degrading alliance, and even Lady Russell felt it would be an unfortunate choice because his profession and fortunes were uncertain at the time and she was so young. Anne was forced to end the relationship, but separation could not mend her broken heart.

"When Sir Walter, who was under financial duress, moved to Bath, they leased Kellynch Hall to Admiral Croft and his wife, Sofie, Captain Wentworth's sister. Anne stayed behind to oversee the transition, but she was distressed at the prospect of encountering him again at the family estate, for she had never stopped loving him and feared he had long ago forgotten her and perhaps even despised her. To avoid an encounter, she went to stay with her sister, Mary Musgrove, at Uppercross, before joining her father and sister in Bath.

"Their paths crossed despite her plan when he visited the Crofts and they all were introduced to the large Musgrove family. Mary's husband, Charles, had two very eligible sisters, who were quite enamoured with the handsome naval captain and, after meeting them, he became a regular caller, much to Anne's dismay. He was still the only man she had ever loved, and she could consider no other. She had even turned down a proposal from Charles Musgrove, who later went on to propose to Mary. Everyone was certain that Captain Wentworth, now successful and quite wealthy from his naval exploits, would marry one of the Musgrove daughters, a prospect that she could hardly contemplate without severe heartache.

"As fate would have it, both the Musgrove daughters married others in the end, and Captain Wentworth, whose heart had reawakened, made his way to Bath in pursuit of Anne, who by then had joined her father and sister. It was during that time that Anne and I became reacquainted. Mr. William Elliot had come to Bath to reconnect with Sir Walter, and when she arrived, she became the object of his desire. Everyone presumed they would marry, but she was wary and mistrustful of him. I had known Mr. Elliot for some time because he was a friend of my husband, and when I shared the intelligence that he had developed great disdain for her father and sister from the moment he first met them, she realised her innate distrust of him was well-founded and did all she could to avoid him. Once Captain Wentworth arrived, love blossomed between them and they announced their plans to marry, which they did forthwith, at which point Mr. Elliot immediately left Bath. So, as you can see, it was a long and convoluted path to happiness."

Elizabeth smiled as she replied, "I had no idea of the complications they faced, but I can attest that not all romantic paths are clearly marked. Mr. Darcy and I misjudged each other from the start and were blinded by our perceptions of one another. I was one of five unmarried daughters of a gentleman whose estate was entailed, with no dowry and limited prospects for a good match, and it was evident that Mr. Darcy considered my sisters and me beneath him in rank. Initially I despised him and misjudged his character entirely as vain and arrogant. That we married for love was as unpredictable as it was fortuitous, and we are very happy together."

Mrs. Smith was delighted to hear this testimonial as an example of matches that were destined to happen despite logic or predisposition.

"Not all matches are ordained for such a successful outcome," she said. "A case in point is the likely engagement of Miss Elliot and her baronet, Sir Thomas Bertram. She is determined to attach herself to him as a means of elevating her standing and securing her future by using all her feminine wiles to achieve that end.

"My nurse, Rooke, is acquainted with a maid assigned to the Viscountess Dalrymple, and has overheard Miss Elliot speak of her intrigues in securing Sir Thomas' attachment to her. She is encumbered by a smaller than desirable dowry and he is encumbered by grown children, some with tarnished reputations, who are unlikely to embrace her as a new stepmother. Living with already diminished financial circumstances, she is determined to secure a marriage proposal that includes a contract to ensure her future financial security in the event of his death.

"She revealed that he recently acquired a parcel of land in the Americas and has agreed to sign it over to her so that it remains separate from the rest of his estate. Once her financial security is in place, she has agreed to marry him right away. She hopes to accomplish the whole scheme before they travel to the family estate, Mansfield Park, so there is no risk of interference from his family. There is no end to the feminine wiles she will use to achieve her longed-for status to be the wife of a baronet."

Elizabeth was able to add legitimacy to the scheme by revealing that their connection with Sir Thomas was the sale of land in Antigua from the Pemberley estate. It had acquired by Darcy's great grandfather and was partially responsible for the increased wealth of the estate. Elizabeth had convinced Darcy to divest himself from the shameless scourge of profiting from slavery and that very business transaction was the reason for his delay in joining her in Bath.

"If Miss Elliot is happy to benefit financially from such an investment to secure her own future wealth, I cannot help but think they are deserving of each other," said Mrs. Smith. "She has no scruples and her true character will reveal itself once they are married. I pity the Bertram family when she enters their lives, but I believe Sir Thomas will be held in thrall for some time to come."

Elizabeth departed, eager to share the intelligence from Mrs. Smith with her husband.

"Can you believe the business transaction with Sir Thomas may soon be income in the hands of Miss Elliot?" declared Elizabeth. "I can't decide whether to inform him of her unabashed scheming or whether they deserve each other."

"No good can come from interfering in the relationship of two people drawn to one another as I learned so well when I impeded the courtship of your sister and Bingley. What are we to tell him? That she used her feminine wiles to capture his heart? That she is scheming and duplicitous? Many a marriage has been formed by such circumstances and who are we to judge?"

"Perhaps you are right after all. We have little to gain and interference would hardly be welcomed. They may be well suited after all as they appear to share the same values."

Chapter 23

P lanning for the engagement party was underway, the guest list was completed, and the invitations delivered. Mr. and Mrs. Baldwin were jubilant over the betrothal and delighted to be included in the formal acknowledgement of the merging of the two families. As anticipated, Sir Thomas had extended his stay in Bath and would escort Miss Elliott and Lady Russell, and Colonel Fitzwilliam's presence was required to represent the extended family connection. Since Captain and Mrs. Wentworth would be attending, it was decided to send an invitation to Charles and Mary Musgrove, as she was the sister of Anne and Elizabeth. They invited the dowager viscountess and Miss Carteret since their cousins, the daughters of Sir Walter Elliott, would all be attending, and it was also a means of reciprocating their invitation to the reception at the Royal Crescent. Admiral and Mrs. Croft were included along with a sister of Mrs. Baldwin who lived in town. Since the guest list was limited, Camden Place was the chosen venue and would be filled with fresh flowers the day of the event. Care was taken in preparing the menu and no expense was spared for food and wines which would be served on trays by servants since the formal dining room wasn't large enough to accommodate all the guests.

Georgianna's spirits were high, and her complexion glowed with happiness and contentment. She was intimately involved in all the decisions for the party, demonstrating a newly found confidence in herself that spoke well for her future role as wife of a highly respected doctor in Bath. She took special care planning the entertainments including hiring a pianist and a singer of local renown. She had no intention of performing since she would be the centre of attention already, as the bride to be, and had no need of exhibiting on this special day.

Colonel Fitzwilliam came by the day before the event to leave an engagement gift for Georgianna to wear on the night of the party, a gold locket that had belonged to his mother.

"I thought it would be fitting for you to wear and someday you can have miniatures painted of the two of you and mounted inside as it's meant for small portraits," he said as he presented it. "I know of an artist we can engage who specialises in such creations."

Georgianna was deeply touched and promised to treasure it always. She was eager to pursue the idea of having portraits painted for the delicate piece. "It's hard to conceive how artists create likenesses so tiny they would fit. Are you sure you wish to part with it? Perhaps someday you'll wish to give it to your own wife."

"For now, there are no prospects and I'm sure that were I to find someone to marry and wished to give such a keepsake to my prospective bride, I shall we well able to have a new one created. For now, I wish you joy and hope to have the pleasure of seeing you wear it," he replied.

Elizabeth stepped forward to help Georgianna try on the locket saying, "Now is as good a time as any to make your wish come true. Here, Georgianna, let me help you fasten the clasp. It is a lovely gift, and we will all enjoy seeing it worn. I also wonder if you might be acting prematurely. We all took note of your dance partner at the reception. Did you enjoy your conversation with Miss Carteret as she seemed quite animated by your wit."

The colonel laughed as he said, "You women are such matchmakers you will jump to any conclusion that suits your fancy. I did indeed enjoy the dance although I was not at all certain she would accept the offer. I believe she hesitated for a moment before complying and I could not help but notice a look of surprise on her mother's face. I'm not at all sure she engages in the practice regularly, but she danced well and was amusing in her observations."

"Then you will not be disappointed that we've invited them to the engagement party. It seemed appropriate, since Miss Elliott will have her baronet in tow, they will find joining our party supportable for their social standing."

"Is this a conspiracy to find me a wife? Are engagements infectious? When one has been announced, it needs must be followed by another?"

Elizabeth laughed and said, "Indeed you are right. I have it on good authority that Miss Elliott and Sir Thomas Bertram may soon be engaged. Have you not noticed how he has lingered here in Bath well past his original plans?"

"I cannot say I am surprised for I understand he spends a great deal of time visiting at Lady Russell's and when we last spoke, he expressed his great admiration for Miss Elliot, and I must admit he does seem smitten. Whirlwind romances have been known to happen and it appears she may be more eager to marry now as a means of increasing her social status, while she was less inclined when her father was still alive. Sir Thomas is lonely since losing his wife and it seems a good match if she finds his family welcoming."

The day of the party Mr. and Mrs. Baldwin and their sons arrived ahead of the other guests so that they could share the responsibilities as co-hosts of the celebration for the young couple. The Musgroves accompanied the Wentworths and arrived early because Mary was eager to see Camden Place again. She had not been there since the death of her father and entered in excellent spirits and offered enthusiastic congratulations to the young couple. She was eager to reacquaint herself with her cousins, the viscountess and Miss Carteret as well as to meet Sir Thomas Bertram. The Crofts soon joined the party followed by Colonel Fitzwilliam. When Miss Elliot arrived, she led the way followed by Lady Russell and Sir Thomas. The last to arrive were the Dowager Viscountess Dalrymple and her daughter, the Honourable Miss Carteret.

"I see the drawing rooms remain much the same as when I last visited," said the viscountess and went on to comment on the superiorities of the house, all of which were attributed to the refined tastes of her deceased cousin, Sir Walter Elliot. She condescended to be introduced to the Baldwins and went on to comment on the esteemed reputation of Dr. Baldwin.

"I have heard exceedingly high praise of you, Dr. Baldwin, and am gratified by the care and consideration you showed Sir Walter when he fell ill. You are a fortunate man to win the heart of Miss Darcy for I understand she has superior connections, and I rejoice in your happiness."

With that, the viscountess was invited to take a seat and to enjoy the festivities to whatever degree she was inclined. Elizabeth Elliot attached herself to Sir Thomas for the entirety of the evening taking special pride in introducing him to her sister, Mary, and commenting on how much he resembled their father in such a way that Mary had no choice but to agree. When Mary asked how long he had been visiting in Bath, his extended stay was explained as a desire to provide mutual consolation to Miss Elliot, for whom the pain of loss was still acute, as was his own from the loss of his wife. The ever-present linen handkerchief was produced by Elizabeth to dab her eyes and gaze with admiration at the baronet.

Miss Carteret exercised her duties to congratulate the happy couple and their families and reluctantly made an effort at engaging in small talk with Mary Musgrove, who was determined to carry on a conversation about the importance of her being included in the party, since she was intimately acquainted with Dr. Baldwin's ministrations on behalf of her late father, and therefore should not have been excluded when her sisters had already been invited. She lingered on the topic of the kindnesses shown to her sister, Elizabeth, while visiting

Ireland during her bereavement, also mentioning that she and her husband longed to visit their estate someday.

When Miss Carteret finally disengaged with Mary and took a seat, Colonel Fitzwilliam asked if he could join her, and they struck up a conversation about his visits to Ireland and his favourite amusements when he travelled there.

"Are you an outdoorsman who favours pursuits such as hunting?" she asked. "Do you enjoy riding to hounds and chasing frightened stags and beleaguered foxes?"

"I enjoy riding for pleasure and exercise but confine myself to angling for a fat trout when it comes to such pursuits. I don't care for crashing through the countryside with a group of riders and disrupting the locals while in pursuit of the hunted. Ireland has such beautiful countryside that I'm as happy to amble as I am to ride for enjoyment. Do you ride?"

"I prefer to walk and read but occasionally ride," she replied.

"What are your reading enjoyments? Novels? Philosophy? *Fordyce's Sermons*?"

The mention of *Fordyce's Sermons* brought a slight smile and shake of Miss Carteret's head. "I take little interest in the conceit of men to give instruction to young women on how to behave, and to comply to rules over which they have no say."

"You have an independent mind, I surmise. So, what are your reading amusements?"

"I don't think of them as amusements. Reading should uplift the mind, challenge your thinking, reveal new insights. I am particularly fond of history but, since it is written by men, a woman must consider the framer of the account, and realise that the situations and outcomes reflect the values of the writers. Little is said of women's influence or perspective in history. I quite enjoy reading about the reign of Queen Elizabeth because I admire her control, influence, and ability to survive in a man's world."

"So, you think women have been overlooked by historians?"

"Overlooked? More to the point, they were suppressed by male religious authorities over the centuries. Educated women and women of property were often targets for accusations of witchcraft, making for easy condemnation against those who dared show independence. Their property could be confiscated if they chose not to marry, and their education was often very limited. Even now there is no role for an educated woman in society; we must follow our own pursuits as best we can, or society will condemn us to ignorance. Queen Elizabeth was highly educated and multi-lingual, but she was the exception not the rule and barely survived to ascend the throne, let alone withstand the intrigues against her during her reign."

"Queen Elizabeth was known to be harsh with her own sex as Mary, Queen of Scots came to know," he replied.

"That may be but there is some evidence of her tolerance of her female enemies at least in Ireland. Grace O'Malley was an Irish noblewoman and pirate queen who led a rebellion against the English, and she met the queen in 1593 to discuss Irish independence and negotiate the release of her sons. It was not only unprecedented, but she lived to tell the story. She was around 63 years of age at the time of the meeting and hailed from Clare Island.

"Her father was chief of the O'Malley clan, a seafaring people. When her father refused to allow her to travel with him on a trading expedition to Spain, she cut her hair and snuck on board anyway. She travelled with him thereafter. When he died, she inherited his ships, lands, and titles and demonstrated her leadership controlling the coast of western Ireland with as many as five and twenty ships for forty years. She led raids from Donegal to Waterford and was known as the Pirate Queen of Connacht ruling the seas and taxing shipping vessels. When a new English governor was appointed, he was finally able to capture Grace's sons, so she sailed to London to negotiate their release with Queen Elizabeth.

"It's said she refused to kneel to the queen and even complained to her that Irish widows including herself seldom received their inheritance. In exchange for her sons' release, Grace agreed to stop supporting the rebellions of the Irish lords and the queen agreed to replace the English governor who had hunted the pirate queen for over ten years. It's not the sort of tale that many male historians would bother to write, about a powerful and respected female leader. It's mainly part of local lore although there are records in England about that meeting."

"I cannot argue with your view of history if our historians have never told us about this pirate queen; it's not the type of story one even expects to hear and it's quite fascinating. How did you learn of it?"

"I study history and languages which requires me to frequent the Trinity Library in Dublin for my research. What interests do you pursue?" asked Miss Carteret.

"I must confess that I am partial to poetry," he replied.

"What draws you to the writings of poets? Impassioned feelings and tender hearts, wretchedness and longing, sagas of Odyssean travels, love sonnets?"

"It depends upon my mood of the moment, but I will admit I've turned to Homer for adventure and am a fan of the works of Shakespeare. I enjoy visiting Ireland because it seems there is a poet on every corner, if not tipping a pint at the local pub. I admire the spontaneity of such performances."

To this Miss Carteret replied, "You will find the heart of Ireland in the voices of its poets."

Their discussion was interrupted by the need for toasting the happy couple and expression of the well wishes by the various family members on both sides. When the speeches were concluded, cake was served, and the attendees slowly made their leave. When they finally retreated to their room at the end of the evening, Elizabeth commented to Darcy that the event may be the catalyst for other engagements, particularly Kitty and Tom Baldwin and Sir Thomas and Miss Elliot. To this he replied that after observing the conversation between Colonel Fitzwilliam and Miss Carteret, his cousin may have met his match as well, for he had been quite engrossed in their discussion, and it seemed that so had she.

Chapter 24

Elizabeth received an invitation from Lady Russell to join her for lunch with Miss Elliot and her two sisters, for Mary Musgrove was still in town. Elizabeth was quite taken by the idea of observing the three sisters together in a smaller gathering, for while she had great admiration for Anne, she was curious to see her interactions with the other two. The conversation consisted of the usual polite topics of fashion, shopping, and entertainments until a subject close to Miss Elliot's heart was broached.

Mary commented on the gentlemanly appearance and graceful manners of Sir Thomas Bertram and asked how he came to make their acquaintance. Elizabeth replied that he had past business dealings with Mr. Darcy and, knowing they were visiting Bath, decided to call on them on his way back to his home from Bristol. He was expecting to visit for only a week, but his plans had extended to well beyond a fortnight. Miss Elliot interjected that she was the reason for his change of plans.

"He is quite besotted with me which was exactly my intention. I am done with impoverished living and being looked down upon as an old maid. Sir Thomas is a very eligible widower and gave me reason to believe that the size of my dowry was not of concern. He described his first wife as being very pretty, an attribute with which I am richly endowed, and, despite her modest dowry, he decided to make her his wife. This helped raise the opportunities for her two sisters to marry well, but apparently one threw away her chance and married beneath her, and the other found a match with a local clergyman who was closely aligned to the Bertram family, and she still lives near them.

"He confided that his oldest daughter was involved in a scandalous affair, divorced by her husband, and now resides in a cottage with her Aunt Norris, the widow of the clergyman whose living had been Mansfield Park. Keeping them at a distance will be no difficulty whatsoever, I assure you. He was very concerned that this stain on the family's reputation would dissuade me from accepting his offer, but I assured him that one must learn to accept the unfortunate choices made by an errant daughter, when it is beyond the control of a devoted parent.

"His eldest son and heir, Tom, is another story entirely. His extravagant living forced Sir Thomas to discharge his debts at the expense of his younger brother, Edmund, who should have inherited the living from Mr. Norris, but he now possesses a lesser appointment instead of the original preferment. I foresaw some distress dealing with such an unrepentant scoundrel who would drain the family fortune for his own selfish pursuits. On this matter, I simply had to take a stand.

"Sir Thomas knows how ill-treated I have been at the hands of William Elliot and his hateful wife, Penelope Clay, who now dares call herself Lady Elliot. My own diminished financial circumstances would leave me extremely vulnerable at the hands of his heir, and that he should predecease me because of our age difference seems likely. To this I sought assurances for my financial protection and have been abundantly blessed. Sir Thomas has arranged to give me an income that is independent of his estate. He recently acquired additional property in Antigua which will be signed over to me. Once that is in place, my future will be secure, and we shall marry immediately, for I have no intention of travelling to Mansfield Park unless we are man and wife. I want no interference from his children until I am safely ensconced as the wife of a baronet.

"As for the other two of his offspring, the second daughter is married and hopefully, honouring the vows she took, unlike her sister, and his second son, Edmund, is married to his cousin Fanny. Her low birth and the poverty of her family forced the Bertrams to take her in at a young age and she eventually managed to capture the heart of her cousin. They should be easily managed once they see how happy I make their father. So, there you have it. I shall soon be the wife of Sir Thomas Bertram, Baronet of Mansfield Park. Oh, how I relish the thought. Fie on William Elliot and that creature he calls his wife."

No one was sure how to respond to this exposition. Ordinarily, congratulations would be in order, but this account of their courtship left little doubt as to the nature of the match, love on the one hand and commerce on the other.

Finally, Mary spoke up. "Do you have feelings for Sir Thomas? Are you ready for the responsibilities of being his wife?"

"He is still handsome enough, so I needn't be ashamed to be seen with him. He has courtly manners, dresses well and although he is besotted with me, I hope that his age will limit his expectations of my wifely duties, and, in the end, I will be financially independent."

Anne spoke next. "It seems likely the property in Antigua must be based on the slave trade. It is such an abominable practice I wonder if it causes you any concern?"

"Really, Anne, one cannot contemplate such thoughts. What care I about people halfway across the world? Fortunes are made on the backs of others, and it is simply a fact that some lives matter more than others, and that is the way of the world. Everyone finds their own level."

Lady Russell followed with a question of how soon the property transfer would be completed to which the reply was any day now. With that an effort was made to express congratulations but it lacked the enthusiasm that such celebratory news would usually engender.

As Elizabeth returned home, she could not help but admire Anne Wentworth as the only sensible one of the three sisters, unspoiled by privilege or avarice, true to her principles, and in possession of a warm and loving heart.

~~*~*

The marriage of Sir Thomas Bertram and Miss Elizabeth Elliot transpired the following week. It was a private affair with limited invitations sent. No one from the Bertram family was invited, although Miss Elliot helped compose letters that were sent informing them of the nuptials. Sir Thomas asked Colonel Fitzwilliam to stand up for him and Anne Wentworth did the same for her sister, Elizabeth. The Dowager Viscountess Dalrymple and her daughter, Catherine Carteret, were in attendance, as were Charles and Mary Musgrove, and of course, Lady Russell. The Darcys were invited along with their sisters and Dr. Baldwin. The wedding took place in the Abbey, regarded as one of the most beautiful churches in all of England, and the bride wore a white Irish linen dress detailed with exquisite handmade lace. A reception followed at the Royal Crescent and the Bath newspaper covered the event the next morning. During the reception, Colonel Fitzwilliam engaged in conversation with Miss Carteret.

"Do you foresee marital bliss and a happy life together for the Bertrams?" he asked.

"I cannot imagine anyone having a happy life with the new Lady Bertram. She is duplicitous and scheming and I pity his family when they discover her true nature. However, I rather expect Sir Thomas may be blinded to all by her pretty face and his confidence in his own superior judgement."

"Do you judge all marriages so harshly or is this reserved for today's happy couple only?"

"I judge marriage as a happy event for any husband because his wife becomes his possession with no rights of her own. A wife is subjugated entirely to her husband's will, a state to which I cannot imagine submitting."

"Does love play no part in the joining of two people in marriage?"

"Perhaps it does but I have seen little evidence of it. Mostly it seems that matrimony is an alliance of financial convenience for the one and obligation for the other. Single women who lack fortune and don't wish to be a burden on their families, must marry out of necessity."

"I can attest that is not always the case. My cousin Darcy and his wife are a true love match, even though she refused him the first time he proposed. He realised at once that she would never marry him for his wealth and status alone, which further increased his desire to attain her and forced him to reconsider his own shortcomings."

Surprised by this response, Miss Carteret then asked, "I'm intrigued. What were his faults that caused her to reject him at first?"

"His vanity and arrogance were the source of the rejection for he made the unpardonable mistake of telling her his proposal went against his own good judgement," said Fitzwilliam with a laugh. "If it were not for her refusal, he might never have recognised his flaws and corrected them. It is the balance they bring to each other that makes for a happy marriage and I do not think she perceives herself as his possession nor does he. They are equals in the relationship."

A smile crossed the face of Catherine Carteret. "Perhaps you have given me hope that marriage can be successful between two people if love makes room for them to treat each other with respect as equals."

The Bertrams were off to London the next day to celebrate

their nuptials before travelling to Mansfield Park. The Musgroves departed a few days later for Uppercross, while the Wentworths continued their stay in town for a few more weeks, as did Admiral Croft and his wife. Miss Carteret and her mother were scheduled to stay until the end of the month. The Darcys began making plans to return to Pemberley despite the pleadings of Georgianna and Kitty to stay longer.

Chapter 25

D r. Baldwin now called daily at Camden Place to see his fiancée for he was especially eager to spend as much time as he could with Georgianna since she would be leaving for home soon. During one of his visits, he found Elizabeth home alone and they sat in the parlour conversing about upcoming travel plans.

"Mrs. Darcy, we haven't spoken privately in a while and I wonder how you are doing? It has been some time since you visited the baths for relaxation treatments. I expected you to visit on the first day of your next monthly course. Are you well?"

Elizabeth was suddenly struck with a realisation of how much time had elapsed since her last visit for the very reason he mentioned. She had not had her monthly course in some time.

"I must admit I've lost track. There has been so much activity of late with visits, parties, the engagement and wedding planning. How long has it been I wonder? I have been well aside from a few light-headed moments and occasional nausea. I feel quite well indeed, although a sip of champagne at your engagement party disagreed with me such that I didn't finish the glass."

"Have you felt any other changes?"

She thought for a moment and then a smile slowly crossed her face. "Some of my dresses became ill-fitting and did not seem to drape correctly. I thought I had put on weight but now I realise that I've noticed other sensations as well. Is it possible? Do you think it possible?"

"I will check the appointment calendar, but I think it is nearly two and half months since your original treatment. It is very possible and the symptoms you describe are another indication. Morning sickness is very common in the early stages of pregnancy, and you were light-headed the afternoon you came to dine at Holbourn. My mother mentioned it and you spoke of it as well later in the day. I am greatly encouraged."

Elizabeth's complexion flushed with colour and her eyes lit up with pleasure at the mere thought that she might be pregnant once again. She began to calculate the days and events that followed her original daily schedule to the baths. After the two weeks were completed, she enjoyed it so much that she continued to go occasionally, especially on days when Mrs. Smith was scheduled for treatments. They delighted in each other's companionship and would often stop by to see Lady Russell afterwards. She had completely lost track.

"Let me write down the name of a local family doctor who can give you an examination. These matters are not my specialty, but I can highly recommend someone who is very experienced and reliable."

Elizabeth could barely compose herself in her excitement and made arrangements that very day to see the physician Dr. Baldwin suggested. Her optimism was justly rewarded following the examination, for it was confirmed that she was with child, and likely three months along based on the date of her last monthly course. She must have become pregnant very shortly after Darcy's arrival in Bath.

The jubilation she felt was equally matched by her husband, but his immediate concern was whether it was safe for her to travel. It was during this same stage of pregnancy that she had experienced the first miscarriage. It seemed so very long ago and so much had transpired since that painful episode in their marriage, but they didn't want to take any chances of a recurrence. They decided they would delay their departure by another month so that she was safely into the second trimester. The news was cause for double rejoicing; Georgianna and Kitty were equally thrilled by her news and also by the fact that they would stay an extra month in Bath.

Dr. Baldwin was the hero of the day. Everyone was certain that his treatment plan at the baths had provided the necessary balm to restore Elizabeth's physical and emotional well-being leading to the happy news. A month's delay returning to Pemberley would put more pressure on preparations for the wedding, but they decided not to change the date lest it affect the timing of her confinement later. It was with a joyous heart that Elizabeth sat down to write the news to her parents and her sister, Jane, regarding the cause of the delay in their departure. She received the following reply from Jane Bingley.

Dearest Lizzy,

My heart soared when I read your letter. I have hoped and prayed that you would be blessed again and I'm sure you will carry to term successfully this time. Little Amy has grown so quickly that I can barely remember what it was like to be pregnant or to hold a tiny infant in my arms. Now she has the run of the house. Charles and I hope to be blessed again, but nothing could bring me greater joy than to hear your news. I do think it wise for you to delay your travel plans for another month.

What a blessing your trip to Bath has been. Georgianna is engaged to a wonderful young man and you've made so many new acquaintances. Kitty wrote me recently and it seems a relationship with Dr. Baldwin's brother may be developing. She could speak of nothing else but the wonderful time she has had getting to know the Baldwin family and I can hardly believe that she has taken up riding.

It reminds me of that terrible time I rode out to Netherfield on horseback in the rain at the invitation of Caroline Bingley, and I became ill. Remember how you walked all the way out there just to be by my side? Who could have dreamed that I would end up married to Charles and you to Fitzwilliam Darcy? Surely there's no accounting for the twists of fate that bring two people together.

Please share our congratulations with your dear husband.
Charles is as thrilled for you as I am. Give my love to Kitty
and Georgianna.

I remain you your loving sister,
Jane B.

The extra month in Bath passed by quickly with much attention paid to the purchasing of wedding clothes for Georgianna, correspondence with Mrs. Reynolds regarding preparations at Pemberley, and small farewell parties as their new acquaintances departed Bath for their homes. Elizabeth had grown fond of Lady Russell who was returning to Kellynch Lodge and she would miss seeing her. She felt fortunate that Georgianna would be residing in Bath since Lady Russell visited annually and they would have opportunity to continue their acquaintance. She was especially happy to continue her friendship with Mrs. Smith who was a permanent resident and had become a real favourite.

The Wentworths and Crofts were also departing around the same time as Lady Russell and Elizabeth looked forward to renewing their friendship the next season knowing she would see Anne Wentworth again. She had developed a great deal of respect for Anne after meeting her sisters and coming to know the circumstances of her long separation from and later marriage to Captain Wentworth.

As the departures became imminent, Lady Russell decided to organise a small final dinner party including the Wentworths, the Crofts, the Darcys, Colonel Fitzwilliam, and the viscountess and her daughter, who were also departing in few days for Ireland. They were gathered in the parlour and enjoying a convivial discussion about events of the season including the wedding of Sir Thomas to Elizabeth Elliot when Miss Carteret took a seat next to Elizabeth. It was the first time she had made an overture for conversation rather than merely nodding an acknowledgement in greeting, expressing thanks, or saying goodbye.

"I wish to congratulate you on the joyful news that you are expecting a child, Mrs. Darcy. I understand that you've experienced a disappointing episode in the past and this is a most welcome event."

"I thank you for your well-wishes, Miss Carteret. It is happy news, indeed, and we are overjoyed at the prospect. I am doubly grateful to have met Dr. Baldwin both because of his engagement to Miss Darcy, and for his kindness and attention to me. I truly believe he has worked a small miracle in my time here."

"I suspect nature would have taken its course anyway, but I do agree that Dr. Baldwin is a caring, knowledgeable, and insightful man, and his ministrations can only have done you good. Miss Darcy has chosen a fine man for a husband and partner who is highly regarded by this community."

"I do so agree with you, Miss Carteret, for he has been a revelation in so many ways. When we travelled here, my sister-in-law was very shy and retiring, but when she met Dr. Baldwin, a completely unexpected side of her emerged and she gained confidence in herself based on her exposure to new information and ideas, which inspired an unanticipated interest in science and history that formed a bond between them. It really is quite amazing, and I believe she will thrive in the relationship."

"It is heartening to consider that young women, when exposed to education beyond the latest fashions, dances, and needlework patterns, can flourish. Conforming to society's expectations of women can be very confining and it seems Miss Darcy has made a match that will allow her to grow and develop her own interests beyond the traditional role for women."

Colonel Fitzwilliam approached to join their conversation. "I hope I don't importune you, but I can think of no two women whose discussion I would rather join than yours," he said with a smile.

"You are most welcome to join us, Colonel, for you can provide a man's perspective. We are discussing the role of women, both the limitations and the opportunities. What is your opinion of expanding education for women beyond domestic training as wife and mother?" asked Miss Carteret.

"Why, that women are the better half of men, and society would all be well served by allowing them to be better informed, to speak their minds, and to trust their own hearts," he replied.

"Well spoken," replied Miss Carteret to which Elizabeth nodded in agreement.

As the guests departed, they made their final goodbyes and expressed wishes of seeing one another again. Congratulations to the Darcys were repeated regarding the expected new addition to their family as well as the upcoming marriage of Georgianna and Dr. Baldwin.

As Fitzwilliam held the door for Miss Carteret and her mother, she inquired if he planned to visit Ireland again, to which he replied that he hoped to visit very soon. Her mother cocked her head to one side and raised her eyebrows in surprise at both the question and the answer.

Chapter 26

Elizabeth's last visit before departing from Bath was with Mrs. Smith who was thrilled to hear the news that she was expecting because they had already discussed her earlier loss and the reason that Dr. Baldwin had recommended the treatments at the baths.

"I have always declared that he is a miracle worker. After considering the improvements in my own acute rheumatic condition since coming under his care, it is a testament to his unique comprehension and inherent instincts for healing. When I first arrived in Bath, I was quite immobilised but after I was introduced to him by Anne, the progress of my recuperation has been remarkable, and for that I am so grateful. He is a treasure to this community."

"That he was able to capture the heart of our beloved but shy Georgianna is yet another tribute. He awakened in her unanticipated interests, a desire to learn, and a newfound confidence in herself, that no one could have predicted. It was most unexpected and her discernment of his excellent character and exceptional merits speaks well for both. Mutual love and respect will always make for a happy marriage. It is truly an unexpected match between two people uniquely suited to one another," replied Elizabeth.

"I recall you once told me that your marriage took a more circuitous route to happiness than most. Did you realise from the beginning that you and Mr. Darcy were uniquely suited to one another?"

Elizabeth smiled at the thought. "Indeed, if ever first impressions were an indicator of potential happiness, no one could ever have predicted felicity in marriage in our future. The first time I met him, he slighted me at a dance. I overheard him state to his friend that I was not handsome enough to tempt him. I was sitting at the time because of a lack of partners, and he determined that, having been slighted by other men, I was of little consequence.

"From that day forward, I perceived him to be vain and arrogant and, for the most part, his behaviour proved out my judgement. At the time he was visiting his friend, Mr. Bingley, who had recently moved to the neighbourhood and was quite taken with my older sister, Jane. Mr. Darcy made it abundantly clear that he considered any connection with our family to be beneath consideration. Five sisters and an entailed estate he determined to be a material disadvantage to us all.

"At one point, Jane was invited to visit Netherfield Hall by Mr. Bingley's two sisters and our mother insisted she travel on horseback in the rain which resulted in her becoming ill, so I went to look after her. No one welcomed my presence except for Mr. Bingley himself, a very affable, open, and kind-hearted man. For a week I had full view of Mr. Darcy's pride and disdain and hated every moment of being there. By then I had developed a decided dislike for him, and it was reinforced by a new acquaintance, Mr. Wickham, who had recently arrived in Meryton to join the militia stationed there.

"He was intimately acquainted with Mr. Darcy because they had grown up together; his father had been the steward to Mr. Darcy's father. Mr. Wickham was well looking and charmingly ingratiating. He spoke openly of his exposure over the years to Darcy's pride and arrogance and told of his mistreatment when Darcy's father died, and he was unjustly deprived of an inheritance that was due. Since it substantiated my already formed opinion, I was open and eager to embrace not just his stories, but his pleasing address and manly attributes. Indeed, I was briefly attracted to this very undeserving man whose character was later revealed to be most shameful and scurrilous, but more of that later. To complete this story, I must also inform you of something else you would not otherwise guess. Despite my decidedly limited prospects, I received two unanticipated marriage proposals that year, both of which I declined."

"Pray tell me more for I am thoroughly intrigued. You were considered to have limited prospects and yet received two marriage proposals?"

"Yes, and they are uniquely intertwined which is why I have to share all. During the early courtship between my sister Jane and Mr. Bingley, our cousin, Mr. Collins, to whom my father's estate was entailed, came to visit Longbourn on a trip of reconciliation. He had it in mind to marry one of the five daughters as a means of making amends for the entailment. My mother enthusiastically embraced the news but, early on, informed Mr. Collins that Jane, his first choice, was expected to be engaged shortly, at which point, Mr. Collins directed his attentions to me.

"He was a clergyman assigned to a living at a parsonage in Hertfordshire under the patronage of Lady Catherine de Bourgh and attached to her estate of Rosings. The pompousness of his civilities was exceeded only by his obsequiousness to his patroness, Lady Catherine, for whom he was eloquent in his ceaseless praise. It was she who had advised him to marry, thus setting in motion his journey of pursuit that brought him to our doorstep. Although I did my best to avoid his attentions and ignore his advances, a proposal of marriage was inevitable and, to my mother's great dismay and my father's wholehearted approbation, I declined his offer."

"A man impossible to respect needs must be impossible to marry," commented Mrs. Smith.

"Not entirely," laughed Elizabeth, "for in a matter of days he had proposed to my best friend, Charlotte Lucas, who did accept him despite my earnest admonitions against it. However, she had her own reasons to consider and I, as her friend, gave my support."

"He made two marriage proposals in a matter of days!" exclaimed Mrs. Smith. "He was indeed determined to acquire a wife."

"To continue my story, a relationship did blossom between

my sister Jane and Mr. Bingley leading Mr. Darcy to make every effort to save his friend from an imprudent marriage. He was eventually successful, along with Bingley's sisters, in convincing Bingley of my sister's indifference and encouraging him to return to London. By then Jane's affections were already secured so she was left to surmise that he felt no love for her, and she had misread his intentions, leaving her feeling exceedingly disconsolate.

"A few months later, at the invitation and insistence of my friend Charlotte, I joined her father, Sir William Lucas, and her younger sister on a journey to Huntsford to visit the Collins' and there I met Lady Catherine de Bourgh who, as it happens, is the aunt of Mr. Darcy. We were invited to Rosings on many occasions for Lady Catherine enjoyed condescending to entertain those of inferior rank who could fill out a whist table. During our stay, Mr. Darcy and his cousin, Colonel Fitzwilliam, came to visit. Colonel Fitzwilliam was truly affable, and his address was so very open and agreeable, but Mr. Darcy continued to exhibit his usual arrogance and pride. I was entirely convinced that he thought me beneath him, always viewed my person and conduct critically, and despised me as much as I despised him. However, while Colonel Fitzwilliam and I enjoyed a genial acquaintanceship, I noticed Darcy often stared sternly at me and he rarely engaged in conversation, although he would often appear on paths where I was walking.

"One day Colonel Fitzwilliam came upon me on one of my walks and revealed to me that Darcy, during a conversation, had congratulated himself on saving his friend from an unfortunate marriage. Now I knew beyond a doubt that he had actively interfered in the relationship between Mr. Bingley and my sister, Jane, and ruined her greatest hope for happiness. I could barely contain my outrage, so I returned to the Collins' and later that day pleaded a headache to avoid a visit to Rosings. As fate would have it, Mr. Darcy arrived to inquire about my health and after much pacing back and forth, he suddenly announced that he could no longer struggle against his feelings, declared that he loved me despite his better judgement, and asked me to marry him."

"That was his proposal?" laughed Mrs. Smith. "I've never heard such an impolitic offer of marriage in all my life. And did you accept him anyway?"

"Oh no, I told him he was the last man on Earth that I would ever consider marrying."

At this point neither of them could contain their laughter until finally, when the mirth passed, Mrs. Smith was able to wipe her tears and ask what reason she had given for the refusal.

"I spoke of his vanity and pride in offending me by making a proposal of marriage that he acknowledged went against his judgement and his reason. To this I added that his interference had ruined the happiness of my beloved sister, which he readily admitted. I then relayed the accusation from Mr. Wickham upon whom he had inflicted a state of poverty by withholding the living that his father had intended him to bestow to the son of his steward. When I finally accused him of behaving in an ungentlemanly manner, he took his leave."

"This is most extraordinary! How was all this mended, such that you are happily married today?"

"The following morning, I was walking on a path when he suddenly appeared and handed me a letter, asked me to read it, and immediately walked away. The letter revealed his view of certain improprieties on the part of my family which, reluctantly, I could not deny. It also revealed the true character of Wickham by whom I had been very much deceived. He attested to the fact that Wickham had tried to seduce Georgianna at a very tender age and convince her to elope with him. Mr. Darcy was fortunate enough to intercept the scheme and prevent it from happening, after which Wickham was banished from the halls of Pemberley."

"Lovely, innocent Georgianna? What a scoundrel he was to prey on such a young girl, one who had known him all her life and would have trusted him."

"Indeed, you are right, but there is still more to the story of that scoundrel. Several months passed before our paths crossed again. I travelled to Derbyshire in pursuit of novelty and amusement at the invitation of my aunt and uncle, Mr. and Mrs. Gardner. Our destination was the town of Lambton where my aunt had lived for many years and it was closely situated within five miles of Pemberley, Mr. Darcy's estate.

"Mrs. Gardner expressed a desire to visit the estate, but I was disinclined for we had visited many great houses along the way, and I would have felt like an unwelcome intruder. My aunt convinced me that the grounds were well worth seeing and the woods were the finest in the country, and so I acquiesced. We were able to ascertain that the proprietor was not in residence, and I had to admit to my own curiosity, so we drove through a beautiful and extensive wood until the carriage ascended to the top of the road and Pemberley came into view. It was a magnificently handsome stone building set in a valley with a stream that formed a natural pool on the grounds. It was breathtaking and, upon seeing it, I could not help but reconsider the offer that I had so casually spurned.

"We applied to tour the home and were led by Mrs. Reynolds, the housekeeper, who informed us that the owner was expected the very next day with a party of friends. While looking at some miniatures on display, we found one of Mr. Wickham and another of Mr. Darcy and my aunt asked me if they were good likenesses. When Mrs. Reynolds learned that I was acquainted with both, she went on to describe Mr. Darcy as the kindest, most good-tempered man she had ever known who had always demonstrated a generous heart even when he was boy. She said though some called him proud, she pronounced him the best landlord and the best master that ever lived which, of course, astonished me. Of Wickham she merely said he had joined the army and turned out very wild.

"As we walked the grounds, I followed a path by the stream pondering what I had heard, trying to reconcile my view of the vain and proud man I had known, with the high praise of him expressed by Mrs. Reynolds. Then, to my utter dismay and embarrassment, Darcy appeared on the path right there before me for he had returned a day earlier than expected. I presumed he would view my presence with anger and disdain but instead he greeted me graciously, if awkwardly, and asked to be introduced to my aunt and uncle. The request surprised me because I thought he would consider them unworthy of his notice, but he walked with us, showed us the grounds, and asked if I would be willing to meet his sister to which I agreed. He even invited my uncle to come and fish at the stream. The next day, we were invited back to dine with his party which included Mr. Bingley, who was as affable and gregarious as ever and very eager to hear news of Jane. Mr. Bingley's sisters were less than welcoming, but his sister, Georgianna, was gracious and amiable, and Mr. Darcy seemed completely changed. I even began to wonder if he might renew his attention, so vast was the transformation.

"A day later I received two letters from Jane with the most dreadful news possible. Our youngest sister, Lydia, had travelled to Brighton as a guest of Mrs. Forster, the wife of the colonel of the regiment to which Wickham was attached. The letters revealed that she, only 16 years old, had run off with Wickham and their destination had not yet been discovered. Our father had travelled to London in search of them and we were urged to make haste and return home as quickly as possible. At that very moment, Mr. Darcy arrived, saw my extreme perturbation, and asked what had happened. Of course, I had to reveal the awful truth of the circumstances, to which he expressed his astonishment, after which he sent for my aunt and uncle and departed immediately. I was quite certain I had seen the last of him after such a fall from grace and respectability for my family.

"We had no reason to believe Lydia's paramour would marry her, which added to our plight, and, of course, our family's reputation would be ruined. I was wretched with distress by the time we returned home, the house was in turmoil, and my mother had taken to her bed with nervous palpitations of the heart. My uncle hastened to London to assist my father who within a few days returned to Longbourn with still no news of Lydia."

"The man who would conspire to do such a thing is doubly a scoundrel. What a wicked, calloused scheme to take advantage of a young, inexperienced girl, especially after already having made similar overtures to Georgianna," cried Mrs. Smith in outrage.

"News finally did come. She was discovered and an arrangement was made for them to marry and we presumed our uncle had undertaken the debt to make it happen. Shortly thereafter, the newlyweds travelled to Longbourn on their way north, during which time, Lydia revealed a secret she was sworn to keep. It was Mr. Darcy who had discovered them and prevailed upon Wickham to marry her at his own expense. I learned all of this from my aunt with whom Lydia had stayed until after the marriage was finalised."

"I know now why this story has a happy ending," smiled Mrs. Smith.

"Indeed, you are correct. Shortly after the scandal passed, Mr. Bingley and Mr. Darcy returned to the neighbourhood and Jane was soon engaged. My happiness was almost complete."

"But was there not a third proposal to you?"

"Not exactly. We all went walking one day and I took the opportunity to reveal to Mr. Darcy that I was aware of what he had done on behalf of our family so that I could thank him. Instead he claimed that he had done it only for me, that his feelings for me were the same as ever, and asked if my feelings for him had changed, which, of course, they had. In fact, they were completely the opposite. That very day he applied to my father, who was shocked that I would even consider the match and I had to protest to him that Mr. Darcy was not the prideful person I had first known and to admit that my own prejudices against him had been tempered as I came to know him better. We had both grown in the process and discovered a deep and abiding love and respect for one another as a result."

Mrs. Smith smiled and said, "I am so grateful to you for sharing such an intimate story with me and am reminded of the happy years of my own marriage before my husband passed away. To love and be loved is the greatest of blessings and, no matter how you find your way to that happy state, it is a wonderful destination to reach."

Chapter 27

The time had come to depart for Pemberley and when they arrived, there was rapture in the air for the happy events to come, although Mrs. Reynolds was experiencing some despondency knowing that her beloved Georgianna would live so far away. Planning began immediately and the guest list was finalised so the invitations could be dispatched. Elizabeth was glowing with contentment as her body was growing and changing, and Georgianna enthusiastically took on a central role in organising the plans for the celebration of her marriage. Mary Wink was determined to convince them the nuptials should take place at their church with her husband officiating the ceremony and her providing the music. Instead it was decided the service would take place at the church in Lambton that Georgianna had always attended, so that the reverend and a very pregnant Mrs. Wink, could enjoy attending as guests without the pressure of performing.

Kitty returned to Longbourn to visit with her parents and

share the news of her excursion to Bath but planned to stay only a short time so she could assist with wedding preparations. Dr. Baldwin decided the wedding was too far off for such a prolonged separation and travelled to Pemberley with his brother, Tom, for a short visit on the pretext of helping with the wedding planning. Upon learning that Kitty had already departed for home, Tom Baldwin made the decision to follow her to Longbourn and meet her parents. As one might anticipate, his stay lasted a few days and resulted in the announcement of his engagement to Kitty. Now there would be two weddings to plan and poor Mrs. Bennet's nerves were all aflutter, along with the palpitations of her heart, and the jubilation of her spirits to have the last of her five daughters betrothed. She made the rounds of the neighbourhood to announce the happy news to all of her friends, her sister, Mrs. Phillips, and, of course, Sir William and Lady Lucas.

It was fortunate that Dr. Baldwin made the trip, for his mother had sent along a list of friends and relatives designated to receive invitations which was helpful to have on hand so Georgianna could confer with her brother and Elizabeth before finalising the guest list and the invitations could be sent. Among those included were Lady Catherine and Miss Anne de Bourgh, which necessitated inviting Mr. and Mrs. Collins; Colonel Fitzwilliam; Mr. and Mrs. Bingley along with his sisters, Caroline Bingley and Mrs. Hurst and her husband; Mr. and Mrs. Bennet; Mr. and Mrs. Wink; and Mr. and Mrs. Gardner, Mr. and Mrs. Phillips, and Sir William and Lady Lucas. They considered whether to avoid inviting Lydia

Wickham, but she invited herself anyway although it was acknowledged her husband would not be able to attend. The list from the Baldwins was not overly long because of the travel involved but Mrs. Baldwin's sister was among those who planned to attend. Tom was designated to be best man for his brother, James, and Kitty was to be bridesmaid for Georgianna.

Responses began to arrive after the wedding invitations were sent including a letter from Lady Catherine de Bourgh that Darcy shared with Elizabeth.

Dear Nephew,

Pray tell me my eyes deceive me. I should think it a scandalous falsehood if I were not beholding a wedding invitation from you at this very moment. Can it be that you have attached our dear Georgianna to a man who trades his services for pay? Who owns no property to speak of? That he is little better than a country doctor? Tell me not that he is a scientist and revered by the community as I have heard from Mrs. Collins, and that he is merely a second son with no inheritance. What can you be thinking? I understand your sister-in-law has achieved a better match by becoming engaged to the elder brother who will inherit the family estate. Would that the circumstances were the reverse for I should not be forced to write this letter. Where is your sense of propriety?

The purpose of a marriage is the preservation and growth of family wealth and esteem. You owe it to yourself and your family to achieve such an outcome; affection is desirable but secondary. You have already squandered your own opportunity by marrying beneath you, but I have endeavoured to come to terms with your choice and now you allow your own sister to do the very same. Have you lost your reason? This is not to be borne.

How can I accept an invitation to bear witness to the union of Georgianna to such a lowly connection? Since childhood she has been destined for a great marriage that assures her the life of comfort and status to which she was born. What can you be thinking? What would your own parents have to say? I am certain my dear sister would be shocked and appalled. Let me assure you that my daughter and I will not be attending this sad affair that brings shame upon our entire family. You must take responsibility for our absence and inform your sister of my grave disappointment in her choice for a husband. I remain your extremely distraught aunt,

Lady Catherine de Bourgh

"It appears we can eliminate two names from our guest list," said Darcy.

"I think it is safe to say that this will not be a huge disappointment to Georgianna," replied Elizabeth. "She would never marry without affection and her choice is based on love not status or wealth."

"I have no reservations about her choice, but I have been considering an idea for which I welcome your advice. Lady Catherine does make a point about a lack of property that I have also been contemplating. What do you think of our purchasing Camden Place for them as a wedding gift? James already owns a small house in town near the baths which he can continue to use as an office. Camden Place is a prestigious location and spacious enough to accommodate them and occasional guests. There is a sizeable room downstairs across from the kitchen with large windows overlooking the garden that could serve as his laboratory. Her dowry and his income will amply cover their expenses and they could retain the cook, the housemaid, and the manservant. That would free up the cottage at Holbourn for Tom and Kitty when they marry. What say you to the idea?"

"I'm overcome," replied Elizabeth. "It's an extraordinary gift and I'm sure they would embrace the idea with great approbation. It would be so much more convenient for James to do his research and have his practice in town. Do you think Sir William Elliot would agree to sell it?"

"I don't believe they have any attachment to the location and would be open to the suggestion. I'll reach out to Mr. Shepherd to make inquiries, but I see no impediment for coming to terms. We'll wait to tell Georgianna and James until we have a response to make sure they're in agreement with the scheme before we proceed."

"Georgianna is the luckiest sister in the world, my love, and I am the luckiest of wives. I dare say, Kitty and Tom will embrace the plan as well. As a young married couple, they'll want privacy if they're to live on the estate. You have my highest approbation for conjuring this idea although perhaps Lady Catherine provided some additional motivation, just so you can prove her claims about a lack of property wrong. For that we can be grateful and perhaps even thank her."

It would be difficult to say which couple was more thrilled

with the gifting of Camden Place as a wedding present, James and Georgianna or Tom and Kitty. The plan was eagerly embraced and gratefully accepted. Mr. Shepherd negotiated an agreement with Sir William and the transfer of property was underway. When James and Georgianna returned to Bath, they would be the proud owners of a lofty and dignified home of consequence that exactly suited their needs. Most auspicious of all was the friendship of the two young women would be uninterrupted by distance that often separates dear friends and they would be united more closely than ever in marriage.

The brothers Baldwin arrived along with their parents and aunt a few days ahead of the ceremony. Mr. and Mrs. Baldwin were a bit incredulous when they first viewed Pemberley, but they soon recovered and made for charming guests at the small parties that preceded the nuptials. Mrs. Baldwin was so congenial that she made for amiable company among her new acquaintances and delighted everyone. They were overwhelmed with the news of the purchase of Camden Place for James and Georgianna and eagerly embraced the idea of refurbishing the cottage for Tom and Kitty who would soon be living there. Their sons had chosen wisely and propitiously.

The day of the wedding arrived, and they made their way to the parsonage at Lambton for the ceremony where Darcy walked his sister down the aisle. The church was beautifully decorated with fresh flowers; the bride was elegantly dressed and glowing with happiness; her brother beamed with pride standing next to his noticeably pregnant wife; Mr. Collins was inordinately gratified that he and his wife were invited despite the misgivings of Lady Catherine; Mr. and Mrs. Bingley undertook to control little Amy so she didn't disrupt the service; Mrs. Bennet rejoiced that her own daughter would soon be next to the altar; Mrs. Wink still regretted that she was not asked to perform but had hopes for the reception to follow; Caroline Bingley made less than subtle efforts to capture the attention of Colonel Fitzwilliam throughout the event; and Lydia Wickham proudly declared herself to be the youngest of the five sisters but the first to marry.

"Oh, Mr. Bennet, hasn't our Lizzy done us a great service finding husbands for her sisters? I always said that if one of our girls married well, it would create opportunities for the others to do likewise."

"Indeed, she has, Mrs. Bennet. She has been an excellent matchmaker. I do believe that if we had produced a sixth daughter, Lizzy would have her married off as well. We owe you both congratulations and our thanks, my dear," said Mr. Bennet.

"Please, Papa, I deserve no such credit or approbation. I had no ambition to be a matchmaker and it would be impolitic of you to think so. Kitty's engagement to Tom Baldwin and Georgianna's marriage to Dr. Baldwin were an act of providence, a happy twist of fate, as was Mary's union with Mr. Wink," replied Elizabeth.

"I believe your mother has forgiven you many times over for refusing the hand of Mr. Collins when it was offered," said her father.

"Mr. Collins! Charlotte Lucas is welcome to Mr. Collins. I always knew Lizzy could do better than Mr. Collins and I forgave her long ago, as you well know."

"Please, Mama. Mr. and Mrs. Collins are guests at the wedding and might overhear you."

"It matters not a whit," replied Mrs. Bennet, "for they are happily matched, and I have no concerns whatsoever about their inheriting Longbourn when your father passes, for I shall be made welcome at all my daughters' homes. I'm ever so eager to visit Bath, and Mrs. Baldwin has already extended an invitation."

Mr. Bennet responded, "Mrs. Bennet, is it your wish to bury me first? The possibility exists that you might predecease me, you realise?"

"Mr. Bennet, do not importune me for you know full well I wish us both to live a long and happy life and having our daughters all settled, will add to the felicity of the rest of our days together. We are blessed, indeed, and I still maintain we have dear Lizzy to thank for it, whatever she says about the matter."

With that, Elizabeth excused herself to see to the other wedding guests while realising she was grateful that the burden of her mother's visits would be shared amongst her sisters.

After the ceremony and reception concluded, Colonel Fitzwilliam came to bid farewell to his cousin and Elizabeth after offering his heartiest congratulations and best wishes to the bride and groom. When asked about his plans, he replied, "I'm bound for Dublin, to study Irish poetry. I'm told the heart of Ireland can be found in the voices of its poets," and with a wide grin he departed.

"Do you think he intends to seek out Miss Carteret?" asked

Darcy of his wife. "He seemed very taken with her the few times they met, and they were often in conversation. She really is not so plain as some have said although she does seem rather diffident in company. Perhaps my cousin will break through her reserve and find himself a wife."

"I believe that she is not so plain, and he is not so blind as to not see her true merits. I found her conversation most interesting and informed on the one occasion that we talked. They might be the perfect combination of opposites, one affable and the other aloof, but well matched in intelligence, shared values, and mutual respect, much like we are, my love. At least in this instance I can't be accused of being a matchmaker for if your cousin finds himself a wife, it will be entirely his own doing."

Dear readers, you will be happy to know that a strapping baby boy was born to Mr. and Mrs. Darcy later that year and the nursery was outfitted with beautiful new furnishings. The baby items that had once been in storage, all save the christening gown, had been donated to Mary Wink for the birth of her daughter.

The End

About the Author

Catherine Kelly Hemingway was a leading player in the digital marketing evolution that saw a paradigm shift in how we consume content. She was a global marketing leader for a Fortune 500 company introducing innovative delivery of content as it shifted from print to online and video. Frequent visits to London allowed her to spend time with a British friend who attended the same school in Reading as Jane Austen two centuries earlier and arranged driving trips to Chawton and Winchester.

She acquired a copy of *The Complete Novels of Jane Austen* in a Winchester bookstore which she read cover to cover many times over. During the pandemic in 2020 she conjured the idea of bringing together characters from all six books and felt compelled to write her first novel, introducing familiar characters and retelling portions of original stories while introducing new characters and plot lines. She is now at work on a sequel to her sequel.

Discussion Guide:

How many matchmakers did you identify in the novel?

How and why were they successful or unsuccessful in their matchmaking efforts?

Which marriages do you predict will be successful and why?

Is there a character from one of Jane Austen's novels you wish had been included?

What would the connection have been to introduce that character?

How would that character have added value to the story?

Which new character/s in the novel did you like or admire?

Which characters from Jane Austen's novels did you like or admire in this novel and why?

Which characters from Jane Austen's novels did you dislike and why?

Are there story lines you would like to see carried forward in future novels?

Made in United States
Orlando, FL
07 February 2025

58231251R00146